JAPANESE WHISPERS

In fond memory of my grandmother

By the same author

An Echo of Seals

The summer world changes unexpectedly when a wounded seal is rescued and an enthralling tale of mystery develops.   *(Young readers)*

My Time in the War

Romie Lambkin's diary of her life as a staff driver during World War II.   *(Autobiography)*

Romie Lambkin

JAPANESE WHISPERS

WOLFHOUND PRESS

First published 1994 by
WOLFHOUND PRSS Ltd
68 Mountjoy Square
Dublin 1

This book is fiction. All characters, incidents and names have no connection with any persons living or dead. Any apparent resemblance is purely coincidental.

Wolfhound Press receives financial assistance from the Arts Council/An Chomhairle Ealaíon, Dublin.

British Library Cataloguing in Publication Data
A catalogue record for this book is available from the British Library

ISBN 0-86327-458-7

Cover illustration: Katharine White
Cover typography: Joe Gervin
Typesetting: Wolfhound Press
Printed by the Guernsey Press Co Ltd, Guernsey, Channel Isles.

Chapter 1

Ia breathed in. Any second now, she would see the
original of the picture in the hall at home. Yes. *Yes.* There
is the pink-washed gate lodge beside the dusky avenue.
The tall red wooden gates are open, waiting.

Trees linked their leafy branches above the avenue,
making a tunnel into which the rising moon flickered.
Uncle Krik's speed was such that Ia could not search
between the tree trunks for the shadowy, long-skirted
figure haunting the oil painting she knew so well. Her
uncle's motorbike and its attached capsule, in which she
rode, had not slowed for bend, corner or curve since
leaving Dublin Airport, thrilling and terrifying her like
a Fun Fair Space Rocket trip but lasting longer, ninety
minutes so far. The motorbike swirled from the avenue
to the gravel sweep fronting the house, its tyres spray-
ing pebbles right and left. Uncle Krick lifted the hood of
the capsule, looking like a space pilot in his windowed
helmet. *Garriphouca House* ... at last.

The long, low, capital-I shaped house stood before Ia in the moon's floodlight, every nook and cranny of it stringed, knotted and wrapped into a parcel by ancient ivy strands, double-storeyed square turrets like bookends either side of it. It was no longer a picture embroidered and peopled in Ia's imagination by half-heard, half-understood remarks whenever Greengran came to stay; it was no longer as insubstantial as outgrown fairy tales, but reality. Beyond the combed gravel, a scalloped lawn dropped in folds to a reed-frilled pond of moon-silvered water.

'Ia?' The wide doorway framed Greengran.

'You were right,' said Ia, feeling her eleven-year-old insides beginning to untangle, 'Garriphouca House does call to me.'

Uncle Krik met his mother's eyes above Ia's head. Smiling nods passed between them.

'Good,' said Greengran.

Good also was the hot bath which followed, and the cossetting supper tray Greengran placed across Ia's knees in the old oak bed. Good was the instant, steep descent to sleep. Little else had they said. Neither had felt the need.

Chapter 2

The raucous caws of crows waking in their tree tops rookery roused Ia early. Just as well, she thought, it gives me time to sort things out because all of yesterday was like watching a film, except that I was in it. She hoisted up the feathery bolster and pillow from the floor where she had tossed them last night. She always slept flat. She piled them high against the bedhead and pulled the warm and airy duvet chinwards. Mmm. Comfy. Nestlike even. She felt at one with the crows.

Her turret bedroom had a nestlike quality too, cosy, safe: the only way in was through Greengran's bedroom, the only other way out through the latticed window facing her. She let her eyes drift, taking in the old marble-topped washstand and the lilac-flowered jug and basin which, once upon a time, her own mother had used. The shelves in one corner held the books of that childhood; Greengran's too. Reading them, she would match her childhood with theirs. Pleasure glowed and filled her. The long oval mirror of the wardrobe reflected a translucent green morning light from the wallpaper's oak leaf pattern, but it obscured the content of the room's three pictures by its brilliance on their glass.

One picture was called 'Bubbles', Ia knew that, another 'The Laughing Cavalier'. She was unable to remember about the third picture just now. Ia knew everything there was to know about Greengran's really, either from her, or Muna. It's funny I've never been at Greengran's before, just the same. Only today did Ia think that strange. At home, over the years, it seemed right that Greengran should come to rest with them, in England, now and then. Farming was tough going, although anyone who looked less like a farmer than Greengran would be hard to find with her up-to-the-minute dress style, her lively face made up just so, and earrings always.

'You should see me on the farm,' she would say to their English friends, 'green as grass I am there.'

Greengran's eyes are greener than mine, or Muna's. It's funny that Uncle Krik's are chocolate coloured. Maybe he takes after, er, um ... she looked great in the red sweater and green cord jeans last night, and those little owl earrings ... Uncle Krik does the actual *farming*, well, when he's not too busy taking cars and motorbikes apart and sticking them back together somehow to make new ones. Ia heard Muna say that more than once. She *is* a bit sarcastic about Uncle Krik sometimes. I suppose because *she* works so hard she is not very patient with people who don't, like me when my home-work gets behind. Anyway, Uncle Krik has Douglas to help him. Douglas has been Greengran's chief farm-hand practically forever, from what she says, and some other men come from the village, too.

Poor Muna, she is really slaving now that Dad's redundant, not that she seems to mind. 'What's the use of being Cordon Bleu if I can't support all of us?' she said, 'and Dad being redundant is a stroke of luck because now he can find out if he *is* "the greatest writer of all time".' It was funny the way Muna waved Dad's arm in the air like umpires do with those horrible fat wrestlers on TV. And then Dad pretending to draw his biro from a scabbard, as if he was the Count of Monte Cristo, or somebody, yelling: 'Watch out! The pen is mightier than the sword!'

There was just one tiny snag — Ia's parents thought they were being unfair to her. 'It will work all right when you are at school, but I'm not sure about the holidays,' Muna kept saying, gnawing her bottom lip. Then Greengran fixed everything. Send Ia to Garri-phouca for the holidays, she wrote, starting with Easter. So here I am. But I'm not certain even now that Muna likes the idea one hundred per cent. An alteration in the play of light slowed Ia's thoughts, pulling her attention to the third picture, spotlit by sudden sunshine.

A man's portrait stared at her, a smile quirking the corners of his lips, a cheeky golden beard jutting his chin, his eyes large, dark. Ia met his gaze, disconcerted. His old-fashioned peaked cap and black blazery jacket conjured up a sea-going connection, confirming some-thing Muna had let drop one day, that her father had sailed the seven seas before he met and married Green-gran. So that's what Greengranpa looked like. Funny

Greengran never mentions him at all. Not ever. 'And you're not to either, Ia.' Muna made that clear a long time ago. In a way, it had been satisfyingly mysterious to have a missing Irish grandfather or, to be exact, not to have one. It was only yesterday morning, whizzing along the motorway to Manchester Airport that Ia found there was more to it than that.

'We must tell her before she goes, Muna, it's only fair,' Dad said, all of a sudden. 'You or me?'

'You,' Muna's lips pursed, unusually.

Dad rushed into the story as if he was wound up. 'One day,' he said, 'Greengran and Greengranpa went on a day's expedition to the Japanese Gardens, in *Great* Greengranpa's pony and trap, their two children with them. Muna ('Me', said Muna, as if Ia did not know) and Krik.'

'What d'ye mean, Japanese Gardens?' Ia interrupted. 'I thought all this was happening in Ireland.' Was Dad mixing it up with one of his own stories?

'Oh, yes, I forgot to explain ... hang on until I pass this container lorry ... there! Of course, this was in Ireland, and not far from Garriphouca either, only seven or eight miles. The Japanese Gardens are famous nowadays but then they did not even exist, not until the local lord-of-the-manor started up the whole thing after a trip he made to Japan. He was amazed by the gardens there, the way the Japanese made them into works of art, everything in them planned to be serene and beautiful, places to *think* in as well as rest. Well, believe it or not, Lord Thinggummy fixed up with a top Japanese garden architect to travel back with him to create a Japanese garden on *his* estate. He must have been a rich man because forty-odd gardeners had to come, too, and a boat-load of plants and bushes and trees, not to mention all the bits and pieces they needed to make the men feel at home in a strange country. The whole operation took several years.' Pete drew breath. 'Now do you see?'

'Go on,' said Muna.

'Yes, well, let me think ... ah ... well, yes, after a while, the Gardens were opened to the public, and your grand-parents — they were only parents then — were very keen to go. It was early spring.' ('This time of year,' said Muna, 'just right for a picnic and Teresa, a girl from the village came too, to help with us the children').

'Who is telling the story, you or me? Anyway, it was mid-morning when they got there. Teresa put the pony to graze in a field nearby and Muna's father unhooked the pram thing from the pony trap. Teresa was to wheel the toddlers up the lane in it while they went into the Japanese Gardens.' ('Watch your speed!' cried Muna.) 'I'm not going fast, it's the M62 we're on, you know. Let me get on with the story, Muna. OK?'

'Anyway, Ia, the Gardens charmed your grand-parents, the wandering in-and-out stream, tiny bridges, water-walks and stepping-stones, all the dwarf bonsai trees and stone lanterns, the Island of Joy and Wonder, the Well of Wisdom, the Tea House, et cetera, et cetera. The layout of the Gardens is supposed to illustrate the various stages of life everyone goes through, by the way. The two of them acted out each step of it and became a more thoughtful couple than they had been going in. But one circuit was not enough, oh no, after lunch, they meant to go back. Then Muna's father said: "Oh, blow," or something like that, "I left that booklet we bought about the Gardens on the Tea House table. We could do with reading it more carefully, couldn't we? I'll nip off and get it. I won't be a minute".'

'And that,' said Muna, 'was that. He was never seen again.'

'What do you *mean* he was never seen again?' Ia knew her voice had been shrill, caused by astonishment at the story and apprehension at reaching the airport from where she would travel on alone.

'Just what Muna said,' said Dad, turning into the Airport entrance, 'No one ever laid eyes on him again.'

The hallway picture at home, showing the faint outline of a figure lurking between the trees, suddenly nudged Ia's mind. Now, surely she could ask about it, so she did.

'Oh, that's just your Greengranpa's Ghost Lady,' Muna had answered, coolly. 'A few days before the picnic outing, he put Greengran into his oil painting of Garriphouca, as a stand-in for his Ghost Lady, and then he painted her out again because Greengran said he was always imagining ghosts. The result is that shadow,' added Muna. 'Douglas told me, years afterwards, that my father saw that Ghost Lady almost every day. She was his friend, and no harm to anyone at all.'

'Which is why the picture of Garriphouca House is in our hall and not Greengran's because the picture *and* the Japanese Gardens *and* Greengranpa all tangled together in her mind. She could bear no more, wanted all of them out of it. At least, *she* didn't. Shock did.'

Ia stretched and yawned. Dad had just about finished the story before we reached the flight check-in desk. What a send-off that was! Just the same, they could have told me long ago. Don't they trust me, or what?

A stifled scream penetrated the heavy wooden door separating the two bedrooms, abruptly halting her circling thoughts.

Greengran!

Chapter 3

Ia leapt to the door, jerked it open, feeling her cheeks cold, tissue-paper white. She stared at her grandmother.

'Oh!' Greengran said, sitting as straight as a stick in her bed. 'Nothing to worry about. I do that every now and then this time of year, I'm told. I ought to have warned you last night, I suppose, except I never thought of it. It's a nuisance if it alarms anyone else, but that's all. I just find myself awake like this, and then I know I've done it again.' She threw off the quilt and jumped up in a single movement, giving Ia a happy-go-lucky grin.

'Oh,' said Ia.

'Take no notice another time.' Greengran moved to the dark-oak dressing table. 'Let's see.' She browsed over a mosaic box chock-a-block with earrings, picked out a pair of silver roses and thrust their stems expertly through each pierced earlobe. 'And I never said a word about Tully last night either, did I?' Without even looking, she slid little wing nuts onto the earrings' stems on the reverse side of her ears.

Such skill fascinated Ia. 'What's Tully?' she asked.

'Tully's a who — as a matter of fact, he's a far-off cousin of yours, at least, more or less, he is.' Greengran reached for a bottle of creamy pink lotion. 'His parents had to go to America last week. They're mixed up in an Irish Arts and Crafts publicity campaign over there — Tully's father has his own little pottery works behind the gate lodge you saw last night. He's quite well known around here and his mother — Tully's mother, that is — she paints and embroiders all sorts of complicated Celtic designs on to pure silk.'

'Silk?' Ia said, surprised.

'Mm. Most unusual and *very* expenseeve! But the point is, I'm supposed to oversee Tully while they're away. It really just means giving him his meals and making him wash himself every so often, but he won't come here to sleep. He's a very independent boy. I'd be glad if you'd keep an eye on him as well ... I seem to be extra busy these days.'

'How old is this Tully?' Ia felt deflated. She had never heard of any cousin, more or less, or otherwise. Rightly or wrongly, she felt possessive about Garriphouca House and all its surrounds.

Greengran concentrated upon twirling her golden-red eyelashes to a glossy brown with a small spiral applicator, then she brushed the coppery hair capping her head.

'Twelvish,' she said. 'Yes, he must be about that now.' She grimaced at her mirror image. 'There, face, that's the best I can do for you this morning.'

She moved briskly to a husky oak wardrobe beneath the small, high-set window. Ia knew it was there that nine-year-old Muna had seen a fairy sit on its sill. 'The little man never said a word. We just looked at each other, and then he went. That's all.' Muna made the event sound everyday. Bet I won't see him, ruminated Ia, hard-headedly. Although, mind you, the comfortable long-ago feel of this house could make you almost imagine ...

'Wakey, wakey.' Greengran's hand turned Ia back towards her own turret bedroom. 'It's time for that ten second dressing act of yours — you know, vest, pants, sweater, jeans ... voom!'

But it was Greengran who voomed. In no time flat, Ia watched the muddy-white Mini zip down the avenue and disappear in a puff of exhaust smoke. The Farm Manager side of her grandmother had an appointment with the Milk Marketing Board.

No sign of Tully so far. No Uncle Krik either. Greengran said he had gone fishing. For half a second, Greengran had looked impatient and Ia saw Muna in her, or maybe it was the other way round. Greengran whirled Ia round the house before she went, showed her that and this, to a rapid-fire commentary, concluding:

'You'll be all right, Ia. Just grab something from the larder whenever you're hungry during the day. The main meal's at six, and Teresa comes in at two o'clock. She cooks and keeps the house in order for me — I couldn't manage without Teresa at all.' She gave Ia a humorous, affectionate glance. 'I couldn't do without my granddaughter either.'

The Teresa name stayed as Ia tasted Irish soda bread

for the first time, using a little butter but a lot of home-made marmalade. Mm ... mm ... brown and mealy. She studied the round flat loaf, seeing how the traditional Christian cross, deeply cut into the raw dough, made the finished bread-loaf extremely easy to break apart into halves and quarters, so she ate the whole of one quarter. She poured a tumbler of milk from a bulbous glass jug and drank, meditatively.

I like this old kitchen's red-tiled floor, she thought, and the way those brass and copper pans on the wall over there glitter in the sun, the way they've done ever since Greengran's great-grandmother put them there, I suppose, except they're dented and dimpled all over now. She examined the glass-fronted box in the wall's corner angle above the door, inside which black, num-bered labels hung, relating to the push-bells and bell-cords upstairs, which were used to summon servants in more ancient days. Even the big warm Aga oven looked pleasingly old and battered. Ia's memory clicked with the last gulp of milk.

Teresa! Wasn't Teresa the village girl who went to the Japanese Gardens with her grandparents that day? Un-ease sat thinly on her shoulders. I know very little *for sure* about my own ancestors, she decided, a complete reversal of her earlier certainty.

A freezing draught was playing on the nape of her neck which had not been there before. She turned. It came from the door down to the cellar. It was not quite shut so she got up to close it. A choked-off sneeze froze her hand to the brass doorknob. Reluctantly she drew the door towards her. It resisted. Her hands grew cold, clammy. Fighting fear for the second time within hours, she tugged sharply. A *person* tumbled forward from the cellar's darkness, bounced upwards.

Ia's breath rasped. She wanted to run but her legs appeared to be flowing away from her and into the floor like tap water.

'There's no need to look like that!'

Upright now, straight, lengthy and lithe, the boy inspected her, his eyes black as night, almond-shaped. He ran nervous fingers through hair black enough to be blue. A thick, hulky and ragged Aran sweater drooped almost to the knees of his tatty, once-blue jeans. He picked up a small spiral-spined notebook. That looked clean and new.

'Aren't you going to say anything?' He had a low voice.

'Yes, I certainly am!' snapped Ia. 'Who the dickens do you think you *are*? You nearly gave me a heart attack.'

'That's brilliant! Where's my pencil?' He squatted, searching the floor. 'I'm Tully, if you must know. I suppose you're that Ia kid from England?'

'Tully. Oh.' Ia viewed him with suspicion. 'What were you *doing* in the cellar? Don't tell me you've been there all *night*?' She let his last remark pass.

'Never thought of it.' A swift smile came and went. 'An idea though. No, I just got out of your way, that's all. Didn't want to meet you, really. You take a long time eating breakfast, don't you?'

Was he revoltingly rude or devastatingly honest? He found the pencil, a small silver one Ia was surprised to notice, which he used to draw strange squiggles in his notebook.

'What's *that*?' she asked.

'Oh, just my language,' he said. 'I make it up. It's a kind of shorthand, I suppose. Anyway, it takes less room on the page so the notebook lasts longer, and no one else can read what I write, and that's a good thing.'

'Write about *what*? Why didn't you want to meet me? We had to meet sometime, didn't we?'

That *he* might resent *her* intrusion into what was, after all, Ia had to admit, more his home territory than hers (the gate lodge part, that is, not Garriphouca House), was hard to swallow.

'Do you always talk like that?' he asked.

'Like *what*?'

'Like *that*?' Tully mimicked. 'Putting words into italics all the time, underlining them. *See*?'

'Oh.'

'Yes.'

Silence.

Tully exercised a few more squiggles.

Then, 'You're better than I expected,' he said.

'Thanks,' said Ia, 'I can't exactly say the same.'

His laughter rang out, loud and rough, coarse. 'My voice is starting to break,' he explained, 'just when I laugh.' He appeared to be unused to the idea himself. 'Anyway, you were gutsy pulling me out of the cellar like that. I could have been anyone, a burglar ... a *murderer*.' Ia popped hazel-green eyes at him in mock terror. 'In fact, you are quite a character. Greengran's right. I know she is only my god-grandmother,' Tully added, hastily, 'but she did tell me to call her that yonks ago.'

'Yonks! Gutsy! And *you* talk about *me*. I never heard of a god-grandmother before either.'

'You'd be OK in my play, I think, (Tully did not even hear her) as soon as I find the right storyline, that is. That's the difficulty right now.' His fingers furrowed through his thick blue-black hair like a garden rake. 'I'm a TV playwriter, you know; at least I'm going to be. I'm entering that TV competition for young playwrights. I suppose you know about it?'

Ia remembered seeing something. The notion of starring in a television play appealed at once. She wondered if he was any good.

'Has that notebook of yours anything to do with it?' she asked.

'My ideas book?' He flipped it open. 'There *you* are, for instance.' (Who is underlining words now? thought Ia.) 'Small, wiry girl with green eyes and goldy-red hair attacks burglar in cellar. Burglar has heart attack and dies.' He paused, turning back to earlier pages.

'Is that *it*?'

Ia's self-image demanded a more mysterious setting; she would also need a beautiful medieval gown, or a crinoline, a silky kimono, something like that. Kimono. Tt,Tt! Dad's Japanese Gardens story won't go out of my head, she thought, it's going to nag me for ever and ever.

'Unless you've something better?'

Does *he* know anything? Is *he* not supposed to mention Greengranpa either? A new angle opened up. Asking him is not asking Greengran. Could he be trusted? She plunged, decision taken.

'Do you happen to know anything about somewhere called the Japanese Gardens?' she asked.

Tully's jaw dropped with a hard click.

'I'm going there,' he said, 'the day after tomorrow.'

Tully's announcement dispelled the last shreds of mistrust between them. The how, what, when, why investigation into their individual interest took up most of the morning.

Not here, Tully had said, leading Ia away from the kitchen, across the unevenly cobbled farmyard, in and out of cattle byres, name-plated Daisy, Buttercup, Cowslip, Snowdrop, Violet, Columbine, Primrose, Crocus, pausing to allow Daisy's left-at-home calf ecstatically suck Ia's hand right into its mouth, covering it with sudsy saliva, before turning into the stables, where two donkeys, and twenty-two-year-old Jenny, the gennet (one time daughter of a donkey and a mule), sheltered in bad weather.

'Up here,' said Tully.

Ia followed him up the chunky rungs of a roughly carpentered ladder to the hay loft. At the loft's end, a window-shaped loading bay overlooked, on the left, the beginning of Garriphouca's avenue and, on the right, a graveyard of Uncle Krik's car skeletons beside a five-barred farm gate. Tully scuffled two hollows in the old-gold hay.

'Sit down,' he said, poking his hand deeper, uncovering an inviting clump of apples. 'They're "Keepers",' he said, 'from the summer.'

Ia scrunched. Sweet juice flowed and filled her mouth. Faint rustlings brought forth a large tabby cat.

'Perdita,' said Tully. 'She looks after the rats. She's nineteen now and, at the last count, she's had around three hundred kittens.' Perdita nestled on his lap, chewing gently at his Aran sweater. 'How much do *you* know?' he asked, turning to Ia, whisking his notebook and pencil from a ragged pocket. It's a wonder they're not lost more often, thought Ia.

The sum of their knowledge made a skimpy total: the lead-up to the disappearance of Ia's grandfather, the all-pervading silence lying over Garriphouca ever since. Like Ia, Tully had known nothing of this until last week, just before his parents departed to the United States.

'They knew *you* were coming, Ia. Maybe that had something to do with it.'

The story had tindered his imagination to a white-hot flame. Why had the mystery never been solved? He understood Ia's more personal involvement and confusion of feelings, how she was torn between the family rule of silence and the wistful appeal in the eyes of her grandfather's portrait this very morning.

'Mm,' he said, 'I've one set of grandparents dead, so I've never missed them, but a grandfather just disappearing is different.' He looked thoughtful. 'I didn't know about his portrait,' he added. 'Anyway, I have to wait until tomorrow because I'm borrowing a pony from the O'Mara's, which the blacksmith is shoeing today.' He'd ride cross-country to the Japanese Gardens (he had traced a map from the AA guide book) and give them a proper once-over.

'No way,' Ia announced then, 'are you going there without me.'

Chapter 4

Perdita stirred, sniffing the air.

'Krik's on his way,' said Tully. 'Perdita can smell his fish a mile off, even before our ears get the sound of his engine. That means we'll have trout to eat tonight. I wonder how many he's caught.'

He caterpillared his body to the loading bay and peered over, beckoning Ia to join him. Exactly one minute later, a Krik-assembled half-van-half-jeep rattled to a stop beneath them.

'He's not on his motorbike?'

'You don't know him yet, do you?' whispered Tully. 'He chops about from one form of transport to another, a bit like Greengran and her earrings.'

Uncle Krik spotted them as he up-ended a satchel of gleaming, iridescent trout into a bent and battered bucket. 'Plenty there for us all,' he said, and whisked open the rear door of the van-jeep. 'I've another catch in here. Seen heading this way, so I gave them a lift. Said they wanted to see you, Tully. Come on, you two. Out! Join the ranks of the about-to-be-employed. I've a job for the lot of you.'

'It's the O'Maras.' Tully twisted around and swung his legs over the hay loft's edge. 'Come on, Ia,' he said, 'drop down.'

Ia drew back. '*I'm* not jumping down there.'

'You will. It's as easy as winking. Just watch.'

She watched Tully drop onto an old car seat lying close to the wall which acted like a makeshift trampoline, bouncing him drunkenly upwards and into Uncle Krik's ready hands, and so to the ground.

'See!' Tully shouted.

Ia ground her teeth, closed her eyes to slits, pushed off ... and survived. Micky and Ferna took her measure there and then, Micky in particular, who condemned all females out of hand due, mainly, to a persecuting trail of six younger sisters born behind him. Only Ferna did he excuse.

'That's Ia.' Uncle Krik introduced them. 'Nerves of steel she has. Never flinched once all the way from Dublin.'

'I was scared stiff.' Ia spoke automatically, magnetised by the pink-speckled trout shining golden in the sunshine.

'Anyone with sense would die of fright when Mr Fairley's doing the driving.' Micky was famous for his cheek.

'Being frightened doesn't seem to stop you, just the same, Ia,' said Ferna, who always weighed every word before speaking or deciding anything.

'I need me a coffee,' said Uncle Krik, taking Micky's

remark as a compliment. 'I'll put these in the larder for Teresa at the same time,' he added as he left them, clearly convinced his hard morning's work had now ended. 'By the way, your job is pond-skimming,' he called back. 'Tully, you're foreman. Same procedure as last year.'

A flash of joy united Tully and the O'Maras. Whatever pond-skimming is, it must be good, Ia thought, and volunteered her services.

First, they had to sneak Tully's raft from its hide-out in the centre of a tall clump of bamboo bush, half-in, half-out of the water on the heavily wooded left side of the pond at the end of a soft, peat-moss path, normally hidden from view beneath the birch and beech trees. They perched upon the raft of planks and rusty oil drums roughly roped together and, using a selection of worn-out household implements taken from Uncle Krik's second-hand scrap heap (items likely to be useful to him some year or other), they raked, brushed, scooped and sieved the tiny emerald-green waterweed platelets from the water's coppery surface. Three brown ducks flurried off to the pond's perimeter to tipple-tail after muddy goodies in a more serene atmosphere.

Ages later, Tully pulled up his paddle (a biscuit-tin lid nailed to a broom handle) and threw out the anchor, that is, a heavy stone twisted inside one of Uncle Krik's discarded fish nets. He tied its shaggy rope to an ankle.

'Hey, you've drenched me!' Ferna rolled down the tops of her yellow wellies where the water had seeped in, rocking the raft.

Ia did not like the rocking motion at all.

'Sorry,' said Tully, 'but the middle of the pond's a

good place for talking and, anyway, we need a rest, don't we? Have you fixed about the pony yet, Micky?'

'Not exactly ...'

'But you said ...'

'I know I did, but Dad wants to know what's up with *you* wanting to ride a pony. He would only think of letting you have Dolly if we go with you, so she comes to no harm, but he's leaving it up to Johnjoe.'

'Huh.'

'Well, you're not much of a rider, are you?' Ferna al-vays called a spade a spade.

'No, but ...'

'If you do get Dolly, we could make it into a sort of pony-trek thing. That would be good,' said Ferna. 'Where do you want to go, anyway? That Micky O'Mara wouldn't say.' She gave her brother his full name whenever he overtried her patience.

'Told you I didn't know.' Micky kept on scraping mud from the leg of his jeans with an ancient, blunt knife. 'If Tully wants it kept secret then it's a secret, and I can keep a secret.'

'It's no secret to *me*.' Ia was determined to make the situation crystal clear. Wasn't the whole thing more to do with her than anyone, after all? 'And I'm going to the Japanese Gardens with you,' she ended, 'if I have to ride there on a donkey.' Her body's vehemence unsettled the raft too much for her own liking so, point made, she ceased.

'Oh, so that's where we're going!' Ferna's vibrant-blue eyes snapped sparkles. 'I went with school last year, but it's the sort of place to be by yourself in. I'd love to go again but ...' She flicked Micky a sudden sideways look.

'It can't be anything to do with *that* ancient story,' growled Micky, reading her signal, dismissing it, 'how no Fairley has ever set a foot there since, and all the rest of that stuff.'

'You mean you've known about it all along? Well, the divil and all take you, and you never said a single, solitary word!' Tully looked bitter, betrayed. 'You sure are able to keep a secret, Micky.'

Micky's high, protruding cheekbones flared dark-red: he knew Tully only used devil idioms in anger or distress.

'It's not allowed round Garriphouca,' he mumbled. 'Sure, everyone knows that.'

'Not everyone.' Ferna's eyes slipped from Ia to Tully and back again. 'It's on account of Greengran Mrs Fairley you know,' she said to Ia.

Mrs Fairley though, had no time for secrets, past or present, when she whirled back up the tree-lined avenue to Base (as Garriphouca House was referred to in her business-woman role) and as swiftly out again, pre-lunch, hauling the Mini to its haunches with a yank of the hand brake — the foot brake awaited Krik's ministrations — when she saw them manipulating the raft back to shore.

'I'm off for a fight with Mr Clintlock at the mill,' she called out. 'That man has been damming the stream a bit too much lately. I'll just catch him in time to get taken to lunch, or maybe I won't, but I just *had* to change my earrings.'

The feud between Mr Clintlock and Greengran provided a never-ending serial story which intrigued the whole neighbourhood, the latest episode always retold one to the other with great gusto and exaggeration. Mr Clintlock, owner of the small cotton mill in the shallow valley below the walls of Greengran's property, was too devoted to his mill's water-wheel to update it with modern machinery, but Greengran badly wanted to move with the times, to install electricity, gas, nuclear power, *anything*, but she could never afford to do so, so that was that. As, at the merest approach of dry weather, the little mill-stream could not drive the water-wheel *and* fill the water for Garriphouca House and farm, tempers flared. Every dry spell, Mr Clintlock sent his men to dam the stream and direct its fullest flow down-hill to the mill, whereupon the water ram in the middle of Greengran's kitchen-garden fell silent.

The ram, a stubby, stubborn little iron contraption, somewhat similar to an old-style public drinking foun-tain, pumped water uphill from the stream to the house. Rap, rap, rap, rap, it beat day and night, but no one, except strangers, heard the ear-splitting noise until it stopped. Then every ear took note. That meant imme-diate action. Ia had heard each instalment of the feud's twists and turns since she could remember.

'Which earrings are they?' shouted Tully across the pond to Greengran.

'The little skulls, so he'll know I mean business. Bye.' She shot off.

'As a matter of fact,' Micky nodded to himself, reluctantly excusing one more female, and grunting as he and Tully slid the raft to rest, 'I think Greengran Mrs Fairley is able for anything, or anyone.'

'She's brilliant,' said Tully. He adjusted the bamboo

canes to conceal the raft from view once more.

Their own business called for a jet-trek across the upfield and downfield terrain of Greengran's territory, through the no-man's woodland area of oak and elm, where the fought-over stream bubbled and babbled to itself, past the deserted old beehive-shaped, hunting dogs' kennels, and on into the meadow rented by Mr O'Mara from the nearby racehorse stud. There Johnjoe, the stable boy (who had not been a boy for at least a hundred years, thought Ia, as soon as she saw him), tried to school Dolly and Tully into some sort of co-operation.

'Jaysus!' Johnjoe said, finally, 'I'm not a man for the miracles,' and turned his skills to Ia instead. She was worse. So no Dolly.

Johnjoe took immediate umbrage when Tully mentioned Greengran's two donkeys as a possible alternative.

'Jaysus,' he said again, 'I'm not a man for the donkey-work either. Ferna can learn you that, and good luck to her.' Scorn scored deeper the tracks on his crab-apple face.

Mrs O'Mara's chow-call came over the air like a trombone. Her soup was stew-thick and it repowered the energies lost from the morning's activities. Ia helped herself from a follow-up plate of potato cakes, hot and runny with salty butter, and waved a drippy hand at the silver cup on the O'Mara's sideboard.

'Is that why I kept getting a stitch in my side trying to keep up with you?' she asked. 'For cross-country running! You could have *said*, Micky.'

'Have another potato cake,' said Micky. 'Didn't Mam

say you needed building up with your pale English-city face.'

Mrs O'Mara's dismay at Ia's misleading appearance had amused Ia. Mrs O'Mara did not spare Micky and Ferna's damp and dishevelled state a second glance as she brushed away the half-dozen younger sisters like so many flies, shoo'ing them out to play. Strongly built, in black polo-neck sweater and well-worn jodhpurs and boots, Mrs O'Mara gave the impression that she tossed whatever lay about the kitchen into the oven, or a large saucepan, expecting the contents to behave whilst she got on with exercising another three or four horses. Every domestic short cut possible to take, she took. Plain but good, she said of her soup and potato cakes.

Ia's taste buds decided that Muna's skills could do no better. Mrs O'Mara also offered to provision tomorrow's trip and she cheered Ia by describing Ferna and Micky's ponies as only a cut above donkeys themselves, being slow, old and stubborn. She drew firm lines, too. If Micky and Ferna aimed to be off all day tomorrow, they must now do both days' chores.

'Dig potatoes and carrots, help Johnjoe with straw for the stables, fresh water for the drinking troughs, get sticks and logs for tonight's fire, a few things like that, only double.' Micky satisfied Ia's curiosity as he walked with them to the gate.

Johnjoe feather-footed alongside as they finalised next day's plans above the shrill screams and screeches of Micky's train of sisters. Johnjoe's long hard look pierced Ia like a pin.

'I couldn't be thinking what it was that was annoying me about ye,' he said, 'but now I've reminded meself.

The young Mr Fairley might've took himself off to another place all that time ago, but he's not gone forever while ye're at Garriphouca. Sure, didn't I know him fine and well.' He slipped his scrawny figure through the gate, his steps falling like thistledown down the narrow lane.

'Went off to another place? Not gone forever while I'm here?' Ia felt displaced. 'What's all that supposed to mean?'

'Amnesia,' said Ferna, 'that's what. You know, when you suddenly can't remember anything, who you are or where you live, and you sort of wander off and keep going from one place to another trying to find out.'

She paused, hesitated, then, 'Your granddad's supposed to have got that. So people said anyway. He could have gone anywhere in the world, or even got married again ... or be ...'

'Or be dead,' said Micky, adding, in unusually soft tones for him, 'Johnjoe's pretty sharp about people. What he said means that he thinks you're the spit of the old man, er, young man — Mr Fairley.'

Ia tried to digest that all the way home. Tully respected her silence. Teresa was scolding Uncle Krik as they stepped through the kitchen door.

'Aren't ye in me way?' she was saying. 'Will ye not get along with yerself and do something with your old motor cars, for the dear Lord's sake.'

Ia's stomach glowed when Teresa's plump and ruddy face smiled all over at catching sight of her; she had heard of pansy-purple eyes but never seen them, until now, that is, and Teresa had pretty teeth, if you can call teeth pretty. She had black eyebrows in exact arches but the waves of her hair were as wild as the sea. She was *very* fat.

'There ye are.' Teresa scanned Ia from top to toe. 'It's the grand girl ye are too, thanks be to God, and isn't this the right place for ye to be visiting at long and lengthy last?' She pressed Ia's thinness against her own largesse.

'I'm very glad to meet you, Teresa,' Ia said, meaning it, understanding now what Muna meant when she had tried to describe Teresa's accent, fascinated by it. This comfy, granny-aged woman and the laughing, puppy-fatted Teresa of bygone times *had* to be one and the same. I'll ask her one day, Ia thought.

'Of course, I'm listening to ye,' Teresa said, paying heed at last to Tully and Uncle Krik. 'A day out with the O'Maras? Sure, that'll be the grand thing for yiz all. On the donkeys? The lazy creatures, it'll do them good to shake out their legs after the winter, if yiz can make them go at all.' A hearty laugh shook her second chin. 'I'll have those fish fried to a turn by the time yiz have the donkeys put in the stable.'

~

It took time to find, catch and halter the donkeys. Uncle Krik, when unaided by engine power, moved in slow-motion, lighting and relighting a small, spicy-smelling pipe for a puff or two, and a lean, or a sit, on a loose-stone wall to explain to them, as well as to himself, the mysteries of black holes in space, or the chances of farming the floor of the sea bed, or whatever else his mind was contemplating. Tully, more used to these detours, nagged him on as far as Garriphouca's furthest, half-ploughed field where Douglas Bethehokey was aiming irritable kicks at a 'dead' tractor. Douglas was not silent.

'Don't listen,' laughed Uncle Krik, whipping a screw-driver from his pocket. He strode towards the tractor. 'I won't be a minute.'

Douglas ambled over to them. 'Let him mend the thing himself. Isn't it only one of his own home-made contraptions?' He pushed up his flat cloth cap, exposing a two-striped forehead, the lower half a yellowy tan, the upper snow-white. 'So ye're the granddaughter then?' he said to Ia. 'Garriphouca's the right place for ye.' He wiped a watery drip at the end of his nose. 'Bethehokey,' he said, 'aren't ye the shadow and all o' ...'

The roar of the tractor killed the last of his words. He went back to the ploughing.

The two donkeys rounded the field's far corner. Uncle Krik concentrated long enough to catch them and hold their woolly heads for Tully and Ia to clamber on for a trial ride. Spud, the tufty grey with the bowed back and round furry ribs, fitted Ia. Spalpeen, Tully's, had a backbone as straight as a razor blade but his aged, yellow teeth were blunt so that his nips to every part of Tully's anatomy did not quite break the skin. Once mounted, Spalpeen only resorted to shuddering his whole body unsettlingly, now and then. Spud did nothing evil, just stopped dead every ten or twelve yards with a swift drop of his nose to ground level. Ia found it hard not to slide down his neck at first. By the time they reached the stable yard it was six o'clock and in Uncle Krik's opinion they were seasoned riders.

'You'd better go home and wash up a bit, Tully,' he

said, 'and put on some clean gear or Greengran will
have your guts for garters, and you'll get nothing to eat
either. I'm joking, of course.'

'We won't be able to talk properly until tomorrow,'
Tully hissed to Ia, 'dinner's different.'

His night-black eyes held hers a second. 'By the way,'
he mimicked Ia's greeting to Teresa, '*I'm* very glad to
meet *you*.'

'Me too,' said Ia, sure now of the truth of it.

~

Dinnertime *is* different, thought Ia. In the middle of the
high-ceilinged diningroom full of heavy mahogany
furnishings, an oval table stood on its central carved
stem, dressed with snow-white place mats and linen
napkins in shining silver rings, ready and waiting.
Greengran, at the room's window end, was wearing a
fine wool, crock-of-gold skirt and a frilly necked blouse
and dangly gold earrings, now in her lady-of-the-manor
role. Ia clamped her stomach muscles to restrain her
urge to giggle. Tully sensed the struggle and jabbed her
shin with his toe.

Ia saw no change in Tully's appearance, which she
found annoying, for she had obeyed her grandmother's
hint and wore Muna's Easter present, a turquoise skirt
and sweater. Uncle Kirk dazzled in a brown tweedy
jacket, blue check shirt and a spotty tie.

'Sure, hasn't himself six Aran sweaters, all as dirty as
the other?' said Teresa to the air above Tully's head as
she planted down the platter of trout, brown now, and
dull.

Colcannon, a green-speckled vegetable of creamed potatoes into which finely chopped cabbage was evenly mixed, was no sooner tasted than slotted into Ia's 'Tell Muna' compartment. But she hesitated at the first forkful of trout, their morning beauty shining in her mind's eye.

'Go on, girl.' Uncle Krik watched her. 'It won't kill you. Tully's halfway through his second one. Just look at him.'

Ia raised the fork, tasted, devoured the fish to the last scrap. She hated herself.

Afterwards, it was oil lamps shedding golden light on the dark table and a game of scrabble. Greengran chose words influenced by her meeting tomorrow concerning imported French apples making prices bad for her own crops. 'Krik must come too,' she said. 'I'll practise my French on them, *and* wear my champagne bottle earrings.' Then it was goodnight to Tully and a candle in a Wee Willie Winkle candlestick to light Ia upstairs. Before getting into bed she studied Greengranpa's portrait once more, warmly human in the light of her flickering candle.

'Is it true about the amnesia thing?' she asked him.

Chapter 5

Tully's map showed the way as the crow flies. 'Except we're not crows,' said Micky, and hedges and ditches often slowed their progress. Now and then, a stray finger-signpost directed them. Eventually, they did reach the Rathcur grasslands, where sheep and cattle roamed and racehorses took the miles in their stride as they trained for the challenge of the racecourse away in the distance. So far, the donkeys had kept up with Shee and Pooka, the O'Mara's lazy ponies.

'You might be all right at the play writing, Tully,' said Micky, jabbing his heels into Pooka's ribs, 'but you'd better leave the maps to me another time.'

'You haven't brought your *play* notebook, have you?' asked Ia.

Tully tapped his back pocket. 'Never travel without it.' He flipped Spalpeen's reins. 'Anyway, Micky, we can go as straight as a crow across here, can't we?'

'If we don't start going in circles,' Ferna said. 'There

aren't any landmarks on the grasslands, only little hillocks and gorse bushes. Everything looks the same for miles.'

The enticing musky smell emanating from the spiky gorse bushes' mellow-yellow flowers excited Ia. She would remember today whenever she smelled it again. Micky pointed towards some cars in the distance. They seemed to be driving across the grasslands.

'That's the main road over there where they are,' he said, 'it goes dead straight for five miles, and the race-course is beyond it, so ...' he consulted the map again, '... so, if we go the exact opposite way, we should come out near enough to your Japanese Gardens. Come on, Pooka.'

'Pull up Spud's head, Ia,' said Ferna.

'It's not easy,' grunted Ia, battling with Spud. As she tugged his head up, he jerked it back down, intent on munching.

'Maybe we'd better swap for a bit,' said Ferna. She slid off, looped the reins round her wrist and helped Ia to mount Shee, and threw herself astride Spud. He turned into a brisk-moving and obedient animal at once, slanting an insolent eye at Ia.

'I don't believe it!' Ia snarled back at him, her face flushing.

'This place would be brilliant for a murder mystery play, a kind of hunt-the-prisoner-with-bloodhounds, like they do on Dartmoor, wherever that is. Something like that.' Geography never impressed Tully. 'It's so bare, and it just goes on, doesn't it? Nobody anywhere.'

'It would have to be a film though, wouldn't it? You'd never get all this on a stage.' Micky's mind was down-to-earth.

'What's that noise?' Ia tried to turn in Shee's saddle.

'Hold on!' yelled Ferna.

A drumming of hooves increased to a thunderous tattoo in seconds. Stretched into full gallop, a string of racehorses swept past in a blast of air, jockeys crouching like rag dolls on their backs, eyes wide, dismayed by the unusual, aware of its danger. Pooka's blood heated. He snorted, shook his head, took off, as best he could. Spud, Spalpeen and Shee whinnied and tap-danced, whirled haphazardly, blew out their nostrils in panic, took racehorse strides in several directions at once.

'Ow!' Tully lay prone, winded.

His shaken smile alarmed Ia, still in the saddle, stirrups swinging loose. 'Are you OK, Tully?'

'How did *you* manage to stay on?' Tully ruffled fingers about in his hair. 'No blood anyway.' He rose to his hands and knees. 'Ow!' he said, twice.

Micky and Pooka returned, quiet now. Ferna looked subdued. 'There's more to that Spud than you might think,' she announced. 'He's had me off, the first time since I was six.' She unslung her backpack and poked about in it. 'I'm wondering about the food. Mm, it seems OK.'

'And the soup flasks are here in Shee's saddlebag,' said Ia, 'so that's all right.'

Micky eyed Tully. 'Are you all right? You look all yellow. Here, you'd better get on Pooka. He won't do any more galloping today after that lot, I'll tell you.'

Tully staggered over to Pooka. 'Thanks. The ground's pretty hard, that's all. Divil take that lot, galloping in and out of us like that.' He lifted his foot and aimed for the stirrup. 'Ouch.' He managed to mount.

Micky squirmed about on Spalpeen's back. 'I see what you mean,' he said, grimacing. 'Let's go.' He took the lead.

For a full hour Micky led them nowhere. Remarks of a niggling nature were multiplying amongst his followers when a laneway sprang into view between the hummocks. They clattered downhill towards a waist-high fingerpost.

'Japanese Gardens — 1½ miles,' it said.

Ia pushed her bottom lip insideout and her top teeth gnawed at what remained the right way round. All at once she did not want to advance one inch.

'Yuk! You look revolting. How about this, then?' Micky turned on the 'mad' expression he used at school to discourage teachers' classroom questioning.

'Pack that in,' said Ferna. 'I'm hungry. There's a little parking place just below the Gardens. We could picnic there and there's a good grassy bit for grazing the ponies and donkeys.'

Strong hunger pangs attacked Tully. He was looking normal. 'I'm ravenous,' he said, 'I could eat a horse. Oops! Sorry, Pooka, I didn't mean it.'

The tethered donkeys and ponies drank with delicate lips from a little pool and munched at the grass. Pooka and Shee stayed snobbily apart from the donkeys. Ia stared across the lane to the long and tall palisade of pale wood, a six inch wood-slat roof above it, pagoda styled. Tully saw her stiffen in apprehension. He reached for his notebook, then stopped, thinking: I seem to have known her for ages. No need for notes.

The small amount Ia ate illustrated her state of mind.

The hot soup, hard-boiled eggs, ploughman's cheese chunks, thick cold sausages and brown soda bread sandwiches of crispy bacon rashers drew the rest like bees to nectar. When the picnic remnants were re-packed, they ran to the tiny wooden kiosk opposite the palisade. Inside it, a man was reading a gardening catalogue. He said there was no Guide available this time of year but a leaflet would explain things, step by step, and that would be forty pence each, please, but if they did not have forty pence they could go in anyway; they looked the sort to be trusted. If they wanted to leave their anoraks with him, they could. It was always grand and warm in the Gardens and that is why the blossom and flowers are always miles ahead of the rest of the land, and lasted longer too, God bless them. He gave the information sheet to Ia.

She read aloud from it: 'The seeker of truth here enters the garden.'

Her green eyes reflected the light spring sunshine in the shooting glance she gave to Tully and the O'Maras. With a short and deep intake of breath and a straight-ening of shoulders, she pushed open the pale wood doorway. *The Gate of Forgetfulness* announced the door in ornate Japanese lettering.

~

Gentleness fell into them. Their gaze dwelled on the general perspective: paths, stream, grass, shrubs and trees, graceful shapes and whirls — spiring, drooping, draping, winding — but that was all ... yet. A Japanese Garden's ways take time to learn.

Tully opened his notebook. He was not quite sure himself what he meant as he squiggled: 'Her face is nearly shining.' His silver pencil made quick sketches of gnarly dwarf trees contorted into strange shapes.

'Bone Sigh,' said Ia, 'that's how we should pronounce bonsai, those funny little trees, the leaflet says. There's some only *inches* high, and you can buy them in the nursery garden afterwards, it says.' She was talking for talk's sake, postponing.

Ferna peered over her shoulder. 'That's the last page you're reading.' She took the leaflet, turned it over and returned it. 'That side,' she said, 'and stop worrying. Just because we've come through the Gate of Forgetfulness doesn't mean we'll all be struck down by amnesia and wander off forever like your Greengranpa, Mr Fairley, you know.'

'Dead right. Lightning doesn't strike twice in the same place,' said Micky.

Ferna laughed. 'Guess who has had to copy out pages of idioms for mitching from school!'

But they're not always right, thought Ia. She remembered her father saying the same thing when his friend at the office became redundant and then Dad was redundant, too. That lightning did strike twice. Anyway, she was not forgetting anything, she just felt, well, as if some memory or other was flitting about inside her head like a will-o'-the-wisp which she could not catch.

'Of course, I know *that*,' she said, and read the next sentence. 'Japanese gardens are designed to symbolise the progress of Everyman from birth to death.' She pointed left. 'We're to take this path,' she said, 'to the Cave of Birth.'

'You mean we're not supposed to be born yet?' said Micky, his jaw dropping.

'Not until we've been through the Cave of Birth,' Ia repeated.

The path dipped between chest-high, stone walls. A stone lantern 'lit' stone steps leading down to a small cave which, though cool, stark and dark, had a friendly feel; a fringe of daylight coaxed them forward, up, out, on to a gently climbing pathway.

Micky looked back at the cave. 'I like it. Look at me! I'm just a little bitty baby.'

'Some baby,' smiled Tully. 'But it's,' he searched for the right word, 'it *is* a sort of new-born feeling, and it's a brilliant idea for a play. I can just see how it should go.'

'Next is the Tunnel of Ignorance.' Ia ignored Tully's play obsession. 'It's pitch dark, which is supposed to mean that's the way our minds are now, too young to know anything about anything. Then a light is supposed to shine in somewhere. That is the Light of Knowledge, it says here, and we go up more steps to the Hill of Learning.'

'Ker-lever stuff.' Micky's admiration was total. 'Go on, Ia.'

'Wait a tick,' said Tully. 'We could act it out as we go. You and me, Ia, and Ferna and Micky.'

'She's my sister!' said Micky.

'What's wrong with that? Anyway, Ia and me are god-cousins,' said Tully, 'something like that.'

Ia smiled inwardly, thinking of Greengran's funny phrase, 'cousins, more-or-less'. She remembered something else. 'That's what Greengranpa and Greengran did. Dad told me. They compared it to their own lives.'

'I think,' said Ferna, 'the garden *makes* us act it, whether we want to or not.'

They stumbled through the narrow Tunnel of Ignorance, knocking against one another, stubbing toes on each other's heels, aiming for the pin-prick of light ahead, the Light of Knowledge. They climbed the uneven steps set into the Hill of Learning. On its summit, a tall, slim pine tree drew up their eyes, and up, and up.

'Watch where you put your feet!' Ferna peered over the path's unprotected edge to a ten-foot drop.

Ia consulted the information sheet. 'I didn't read far enough that time,' she said. 'We're supposed to watch out when we're growing up, because nasty things can happen if we don't, and the tree stands for all of us know-it-all young ones, who like to act high-and-mighty although we still have an awful lot to learn.'

They walked down to the Parting of the Ways. The path, smooth and easy (symbolising the Carefree Life) frothed white magnolias, pink cherry blossom and the fire-glow leaves of pygmy maple trees; a second choice, the Batchelor's Way, selfish, unproductive, was more a cleft than a path, with boundary walls of grassy stone. Third and last bypath, the Stepping Stones of Exploration, was a mere passageway of shallow water, shrubbery growing on its banks and Japanese maples and bonsai trees, trained and shaped to frame an outlook, trace an outline, arouse a thought. Stone lanterns squatted. Gnome-like stone figures pondered. This path led to the Island of Joy and Wonder — and married life.

'*I'm* not getting married,' Micky said. 'Come on, Tully, let's be bachelors.'

'If being a bachelor is good enough for Uncle Krik, it's good enough for me,' agreed Tully, laughing.

'The Carefree Life is for me,' said Ferna, 'I explored the Stepping Stones last time.'

The water way chose Ia, her eyes on the gentle water curling around the flat, amber stepping-stones as she lingered midway, the maple trees' new-to-the-world leaves dappling her skin in the sunshine. It was still, except for the shallow water's slow ripple. Again, a memory scratched at the edge of her consciousness, trying to surface. She made open her mind but still it would not come. She shrugged and step-stoned forward to the Island of Joy and Wonder.

Protruding like a tongue into the shining green water, speckled by water-lily pads, the Island of Joy and Wonder beckoned her eyes hither and thither. She tried to absorb everything simultaneously, the purple and pink clematis clasping the pergola perched on the tongue's tip, the stern high hill at its root, the ornamental tree-trunk bridge trailing exotic plants. A scarlet bridge, twin to the Willow Pattern's blue one, arched to the mainland, towards a pagoda-roofed Tea House, half hidden by flowering trees. The Well of Wisdom perched near a shorter, wooden-lathed bridge, where weeping willows dibbled their leaves in the green water; japonica, forsythia and laburnum bloomed rich golden yellows, but the cherry and almond trees were crinolined in fragile white and pink blossom. There was a stone bench. Ia sat down, feeling time had stopped.

An added dimension of light and shadow-play, particularly in-and-out of the pergola framework, flicking, shadowing, was like someone playing hide-and-seek, someone wearing a long gown, more than a shadow ... Ia jerked to her feet, pressure in her head. 'What ...?'

'Didn't you hear us coming?' Tully stood beside her.

'Daydreaming about weddings and suchlike, I suppose,' Micky definitely jeered. 'Girls are always on about that.'

'I was *not*.' Ia glared at him. That girl stuff makes me sick, she thought.

'You're a pest.' Ferna strolled up and scowled at her brother. 'Take no notice of him, Ia,' she said. 'Doesn't the Engagement Bridge come next? Micky won't like that either.'

Micky avoided the issue by catapulting himself over the whole thing in one gigantic jump. Tully crouched on the disconnected stone slabs of the Engagement Bridge, drawing a diagram of it, trying to work out why the slabs did not break apart and fall into the stream.

'*Were* you daydreaming about stuff like marriage?' he asked.

'No,' said Ia, 'I was wide awake.' She scrutinised the back of his head. 'Do you ever have something inside your mind that won't come out?'

'Frequently.' He waved his notebook in the air. 'Why do you think I do this? To prod me into remembering, that's why. Anyway, what is at the back of our minds here is the Fairley story, isn't it? Isn't that why we've come?'

'Oh. Yes. I'd forgotten about it just now, as a matter of fact.'

'Well, we did come through the Gate of Forgetfulness, don't forget,' said Tully.

'I see the joke,' she said, chuckling, 'but it's sort of true just the same. I've been sucked into everything here so much I forgot all about Greengranpa. But I haven't noticed anything likely to have switched off *his* memory, have you?'

'Can't say I have,' Tully replied, 'but a play story plot is what I'm after. We'll make a spine-chilling drama out of this, er, somehow, won't we?'

We, he is saying now, Ia thought, smiling inside.

'Hurry up,' yelled Micky. 'What's supposed to come next?' He snatched the leaflet from Ia as soon as she stepped off the Engagement Bridge. 'Ha, I knew it. The Marriage Bridge. Followed by the Honeymoon Path. Double yuk.' His vivid blue eyes kindled. 'But, *afterwards*, they quarrel and part company for a while, who-ever "they" are. Goody.' He pointed upwards. 'That's the Hill of Ambition, not to mention the Well of Wisdom a bit further on. They're more in my line. See you.' Micky trotted to the Marriage Bridge, determined to get that over without more ado. 'Come on, Ferna.'

'Imagine any girl having to take the Honeymoon Path with my brother.' Ferna made a wry face at Ia. 'You two coming?'

Two stone slabs dovetailed into the solid Marriage Bridge spanning the stream, now running deeply. Ia leaned against the wooden rail, looking for signs of fish.

'Coins,' she said, 'look, Tully.'

'Huh,' said Tully. 'Look at the big silver ones. Are they the old half crowns? I wouldn't mind a couple.'

'And olden day sixpences. There. The shiny small ones.' Ia pointed. 'What about the ones with holes in the middle, like Polo mints? See?'

'I could climb down. There's no one around.'

'You'd better *not*. The coins must be for wishes.'

'I was just kidding.' Tully fished about in a back pocket. 'How about us chucking in a coin? I have a five somewhere, a nice shiny one. Ha, got it.' His dark eyes met hers. 'You drop it in,' he said.

The coin glittered, splashed, settled, nudged close to one that was golden.

'Do you think it could be an old sovereign?' asked Ia. 'I've heard of those, haven't you? Pure gold.'

'I bet it isn't,' said Tully, 'but, do you know what ...? I've thought of something else.'

'What?'

'I bet *they* dropped in a coin.'

Ia opened her eyes wide. 'yes, I bet they did,' she said.

The far-ago young parents flared in her mind until a stronger thought banished it as instantly, yet failed to project its image, tantalising Ia like the lost knowledge of a dream.

'You look a bit puky,' said Tully. 'There's no need to. Greengran is as happy as Larry, you know.'

'I think she is,' said Ia.

'And she likes Mr Clintlock, by the way. Everybody knows that, and there's bets on that they'll get married one of these days.' Ia gaped at him. 'That's right.' Tully laughed at her expression. 'Everyone takes it for sure that Greengranpa's dead long since, but no one knows what *she* thinks. She has never said, not to this day. Anyway, in a small place like Garriphouca, everyone knows everything about everyone, not like big-city Manchester, where you live, wherever it is.'

'Outside Manchester,' said Ia, 'but I know what you

mean, a suburb. I hate suburbs. They don't give a *belonging* feel, like Garriphouca does, I know that now. Garriphouca and me go together somehow. Every time I look at its picture at home I feel that.' She explained about the picture. 'But you've lived here all the time. How can anyone be so lucky?'

'I wouldn't swop our gate lodge for a mountain of those sovereigns,' Tully admitted. 'You haven't been inside it yet, have you? Come down tomorrow. Will you?'

'Yes, I want to,' Ia said. A flash caught her eye. 'What's that?'

'A kingfisher, maybe. Those birds fly pretty fast.'

'I can't see where he went.'

'He won't come out until we've gone. They're like that. Come on,' he said, laughing, 'we'd better hit the Honeymoon Trail, or whatever it's called, and catch up with the O'Maras.'

A waist-high, stone mushroom forced them into single file at the end of the Honeymoon Path.

'This must mean the split-up Micky was talking about,' Ia laughed.

Tully shaded his eyes, squinting towards the Well of Wisdom.

'Come on, Ia, let's get a drink out of the Well, then we'll know all about everything.'

Chapter 6

They could not cross directly to the Well of Wisdom because of numerous dead-ends set into the Hill of Ambition's foothills and, when the summit did come into view, the rocky steps fell away, forcing them to backtrack.

'We're up here!' Ferna's head silhouetted against the blue sky. 'All those twists and turns are the troubles and whatnots of marriage,' she called.

'Huh, if that's what marriage is like,' said Tully, 'I don't think I'll bother. Micky's right.'

'Dead right.' Micky surveyed them from above. 'It's OK when you get up here, though. We're heading off to investigate the Tea House. See you there.'

'We're leaving the leaflet here for you.' Ferna's words faded into the distance.

Ia heard their feet scudding away. The other side of the Hill of Ambition seems easier, she thought.

'Made it,' gasped Tully. He hugged his knee. 'Those

rocks haven't done this any good, I can tell you, not after that kerfuffle with Spalpeen.'

'Close your eyes,' said Ia, shading hers, 'and guess how big the Gardens are.'

'Oh, pretty big. The size of a couple of fields. Why?'

'Now, look.'

Their laughter sounded satisfied somehow. The pale wood palisade was a mere stone's throw from them; so, too, all of its circumference. The planning, landscaping and symbolism within the Garden created an illusion of boundless space but, seen from the Hill of Ambition's apex, the puzzling trails and tracks assumed a clear pattern, at its centre the Island of Joy and Wonder and the dark green water.

Tully read from the leaflet Ferna had left behind. 'We're supposed to be looking back over our past life from here, whether we have been good people, or not so good, and if we've got this far our marriage is OK ... so we're not divorced or anything.'

'What comes next?' Ia's stare remained on the Island of Joy and Wonder, noticing again that intriguing shadow-play between the leafy pergola poles. You could almost believe ...

'We're getting older, that's what.' Tully quavered his voice like a Dr Who robot. 'From here, we're on life's downward path but, if we're lucky, we might just survive long enough for a cup of tea at the Tea House on our way to the Well of Wisdom.'

'Stop play-acting.' Ia laughed at his crunched-up face. 'It says we should pray to the gods down there, at the waterfall.'

'What gods?'

A stone god crouched either side of the smooth wide water, guarding the fall and froth of a twelve-inch waterfall. Tricky stepping stones bridged its crest to the farthest bank where the pagoda-roofed Tea House perched. The Tea House would have looked still more exotic if Micky had not been practising a headstand on its veranda.

'I'm resting,' he explained. 'Isn't this the way the Japanese do it?'

'That's yoga.' Even Tully knew that.

'Oh, well.' Micky rolled to his feet. 'I have to do something to pass the time. There's not a drop of tea to be had here after all, so Ferna's gone to check if the ponies are OK.'

The Tea House had a long low table and cupboards built into the wall; otherwise it was empty. An open veranda circled it.

'Just how Japanese houses should be.' Ia remembered a book at school. 'They sleep on the floor on special mats, which roll up in the day and go into cupboards, not like our beds, and they sit on floor mats, rattan mats they're called, I think, something like that, and they drink tea out of tiny cups, as thin as thin.'

'Sounds like geography is needed in this play,' muttered Tully. 'I'd better move on to the Well of Wisdom. If I drink enough of its water, I might get to be a genius.'

'Fat hopes,' said Micky.

A bucket hung from the crossbar above the Well of Wisdom. Micky free-wheeled the handle controlling its drop. The bucket went down and down. The exertion of retrieving it full of water turned his face puce.

'Maybe it's a kind of wishing well,' said Ia.

Tully filled his hands with water from the bucket. 'I hope it's not polluted.' He gulped once, twice. '*Cold*. Good, too. Wisdom's just pouring in. Have a go, Micky.'

Ia watched them, thoughtstruck. Had *Greengranpa* wanted more wisdom? Had he left his leaflet in the Tea House as an excuse to go back by himself? But why? Didn't he come in with Greengran after all? Didn't they drink the water together, and wish together, like us now?

The little lake below the willows glinted with an odd effect, as if it was catching falling stars in daylight, too dazzling to watch without sunglasses. Ia bent to the bucket, cupped her hands, drank. It jumped her teeth like ice-cream. Its taste tingled her tongue like the silver end of a torch battery. She saw her reflection in the water, shivery from her hands' disturbance — except she did not have a mound of hair studded all over with skewery things, like a baked apple stuck with cloves.

She turned sharply, expecting Micky's next trick. But he and Tully were hopscotching a flat stone on the veranda of the Tea House in a new variation of Shove Halfpenny. Oh! A stab of utter loneliness pierced Ia through. She stared at the water in the bucket, bewildered. Just water. No reflection. I am seeing things, she thought. Maybe those sunspots have upset my focus vision. She had no explanation for the sudden void inside her.

She glanced again at the lake waters outlining the Island of Joy and Wonder. The glittering day-stars had gone. Only the trees shadowed and reflected their trunks, one trunk the shape of a woman in a long gown, whose wide sleeve falls open when she beckons ...

~

'Ia!' Ia's mind mimicked Miss Porrage's acid tones, her most unfavourite teacher. 'You have too much imagination for your own good, Ia Sevenoaks.' The times she has said that. Ia grinned. Maybe Miss Porrage is right.

'Ia!' That was not Miss Porrage. Ferna's call snapped Ia back to now-time. 'Coming, Ferna,' she shouted, and muttered: 'Come out of Cloud Cookoo Land, Ia!' to herself, as she saw Micky staring at her.

'Ho,' he said, 'I thought Tully was the one for going off into trances. You're nearly as bad, if you don't mind me saying so.' Much of Ia still being fairly new to him, he tried to be polite.

'Well, *I'm* not in a trance,' said Tully, and flicked his flat hopscotch stone off the veranda. 'That's it. My game.'

'You crooked article, you did that behind my back. Wasn't I talking to Ia?'

'Ia!' Ferna beckoned from the middle of the blazing-red 'Willow Pattern' bridge, which arched like a bow above the water, its image mirrored beneath. Ia went to her.

'It's the Red Bridge of Life,' Ferna's voice said, softly.

'How long have you been here?'

'Not long. It was just nice being by myself for a while. Micky spoils things sometimes. He doesn't like to be quiet much.'

'I've noticed,' said Ia, smiling.

'I've been to check on the ponies and donkeys,' said Ferna. 'They're OK but we'd better start back for home pretty soon. It's after four o'clock.'

'It *isn't*,' Ia's surprise was comic.

'I know. I was flabbergasted when the kiosk man told me. The time seems to go like wild horses in here. Anyway, the Gardens close at four-thirty. There's not much left to see really, just over this bridge, and then everywhere is flat, smooth and grassy, with stone seats and more lanterns near a pond of waterlilies, and lots of those bonsai trees growing in huge pots, all clumped together, and miniature Japanese gardens in nearly flat container things. Wait till you see them. They're brilliant.'

Ia unfolded the information sheet again. The Garden of Peace and Contentment comes next, it said, where the man and his wife totter slowly onwards, resting awhile on the Chair of Old Age, cunningly made from ever-green hedging, cunningly clipped, shaped and shaven.

'That little mound over on the right with the yew trees is the Hill of Mourning, I remember that,' Ferna said, 'sort of a cemetery. And there's another gate over there, almost like the one where we came in.'

'The Gateway to Eternity, it's called. That's sad,' said Ia, folding up the leaflet.

'No, it isn't.' Tully came from behind. 'That old married pair might be on their last legs, but they are still together and I suppose they always will be once they go through The Gate of Eternity. What's so sad about that?'

'I'm not acting any more, if that's what you call it.' Micky sniffed. 'You're all going on as if the whole thing was real. Gateway to Eternity, phooey, the Way Out, that's what that means. And that's where I'm heading because,' he winked, wickedly, 'I've just spied a little wooden house like the Tea House, only this one has a sign on it with more squiggly letters and they spell something I badly need this minute.'

Tully fell about, laughing. 'Me, too,' he said.

'I *was* going to tell you about the loo, Ia,' said Ferna, as they walked through the Gateway to Eternity.

'Eternity is down that way, and so are the nursery gardens.' The weather-beaten gardener-cum-kiosk man smiled at them, jiggling a bunch of long keys, 'but ye're too late for the both of them, so ye'll never get to heaven now unless ye come another day. It's time I was locking up, boys and girls.'

'*Not yet.*' Micky and Tully sprinted for the small Tea House, which was not a tea house.

The man nodded with sympathy. 'Sure, aren't ye a long way from home. I'll lock that one last of all.'

~

At Garriphouca, before the evening meal, Ia felt flatter than an ironed pillow slip.

'It's anti-climax, that's what it is,' whispered Tully, using a dramatic phrase he had discovered a day or two since.

'You two are quiet this evening.' Greengran sipped her black coffee.

Soon though Teresa's smoked bacon, green cabbage and crisp-skinned, baked potatoes reinvigorated the children: the second course, thought Ia, in Muna's Cordon Bleu language, had a perfect contrast taste, a huge bowl of fresh pink rhubarb and dollops of cream from Greengran's cows.

'You must have had a good day. Did you go far?'

continued Greengran.

'Well, the Rathcur grasslands, mainly.' Tully's milky coffee vanished down his throat. 'There's loads of space there ... we had a fantastic picnic ...'

'The whole *day* was brilliant,' said Ia, 'but I'm dog-tired now. I suppose I'm not used to riding donkeys and ponies yet, and I'm not used to so much fresh air either.'

On the way home, they had agreed to tell no actual *lies*, just to uphold the traditional silence relating to the Japanese Gardens.

'I wish,' said Uncle Krik, polishing the small bowl of his outdoors-only pipe with his napkin, 'I wish I'd gone with you instead of being stuck in that hotel all day, parley-vooing about EU apples.'

'Krik! Sometimes you behave like an overgrown schoolboy.' Greengran's chuckle softened the sting. 'At least, you didn't have to eat any snails or frogs' legs. The lunch was delicious, Ia, particularly the wine. I do love French wine.'

'I know you do, Ma!' Krik's grin aroused his mother's (very faint) blush. Champagne-bottle earrings clinked against their attached wine glasses as Greengran shook her head in reproof; her indignation at the flood of imported French apples upon the Irish market appeared to have diminished.

'Anyway,' muttered Uncle Krik into Tully's ear, 'I like Citroens and Peugeots better.'

'Cars again!' Greengran heard his whisper.

'That *was* one good thing,' said Uncle Krik, 'a fellow there and myself got talking cars. When he asked me if I would like to visit his house in Monte Carlo for next year's rally, I nearly bit his hand off, sealing the bargain.'

The car talk rolled on between Uncle Krik and Tully but Ia felt her head was packed with cotton wool.

'I could do with a stroll, I think,' said Greengran. 'How about you, Ia?' She touched Ia's shoulder, lightly. 'Just a short one before I try to catch up on those wretched monthly accounts. It's that time again.' She nudged Krik as they passed, waited for his resigned nod. Then, 'Let's go, Ia, there hasn't really been much time for us to talk since you came.'

'Not like when you stay with us,' admitted Ia.

'Ah, we've had good times, haven't we? The zoo, museums, pictures, picnics in the park, trips on the trains ...'

'Watching planes at the airport, climbing in the Pennines, drives to the moors ...' Ia added to the list.

Greengran unhooked a moth-eaten coat from the hall stand. 'Put that on,' she said, 'it's sharp outside now, the sun is going down.' The drab coat covered Ia to the shinbone. She remembered one of her father's teasing phrases: anything for a quiet life! 'That was your mother's school coat,' said Greengran, smiling. 'I keep meaning to throw it out but, as you see, it's still there.'

Oh! Ia shrugged the ancient grey coat more closely around her, thrusting her hands into the pockets, digging out a thin, paper-covered oblong in the torn lining of one pocket. *Chewing gum.* Battered, mildewed even, but Ia peeled off the foil, slipped the stick of gum into her mouth, and chewed. *Muna's.*

'Once round the pond settles me after a hectic day,' murmured Greengran. She made Ia chuckle as she described the French Count who kept kissing her hand every time she picked up a sample apple. 'About as tasteless as his silly apples,' she sniffed. They began the circuit of the pond on the woodland path side, bypassing the hidden raft.

'We'll just get through the trees before it's too dark,' she said.

The soft peat path and falling dusk lulled the two in and out of friendly silences, their thoughts dropping here and there ...

~

Greengran: I'm glad you and Tully seem to have taken to each other. Did he tell you about his little brother?

Ia: *A brother*?

Greengran: Oh, then he didn't. A sweet child, Donal ... but *Duine-le-Dia*, one of God's children — that's what that means. Autistic, I'm afraid. He's away in a special school, so you won't see him. I think that's one reason why Tully looks at life so carefully.

Ia: Is it a reason for him wanting to write plays?

Greengran: You've a good deal in common, haven't you? It could be a reason for him wanting to write plays, I suppose.

Ia: Maybe he'll write a play about children like Donal one day ...

Greengran: Who knows? He might very well do that.

~

Ia: Teresa's nice, isn't she?

Greengran: I'd never manage without her, I know that.

Ia: She's not married, is she, Greengran?

Greengran: No, she's not. She never seemed inclined that way, although she had lots of boys courting her when she was a girl.

Ia: Was she pretty then, and thin?

Greengran: Teresa was always what is called plump, but very pretty, and forever happy and laughing, even when ....

Ia: When what, Greengran?

Greengran: Oh, now and then, that's when. Bringing up Krik and your mother hasn't always been easy.

Ia: So Teresa always helped you to bring them up, really?

Greengran: Indeed she has, ever since they were infants-in-arms.

~

Greengran: It's many a long year since I roamed over the Rathcur grasslands like you did today.

Ia: That's a shame, Greengran. You love walking over the Yorkshire moors with us, don't you? I suppose you're too busy, back home here.

Greengran: Mm, I'm always busy. You see that now, don't you? I do drive through Rathcur by road but, somehow, I never stop. Silly, isn't it?

Ia: It goes on for miles and miles, doesn't it? I do wish you'd been with us today, *all* of the time. I do wish that.

~

Greengran: We will have a day out, Ia, probably the day after tomorrow, the four of us. It's time to get the Pool-gorum bungalow ready for the holiday season.

Ia: You've been telling me about that place since I was knee-high. I'm dying to go there.

Greengran: And I'm dying for you to see it, you inland dweller. It is high time you saw the real sea, the Atlantic.

Ia: Nothing between your bungalow and America but sea, I remember. Little sea-horses and shrimps in the rock pools ...

Greengran: And stranded jelly fish after the storms ...

Ia: Portuguese men-of-war with tentacles as long as your arm floating in Poolgorum, the Blue Pool ... what four of us?

Greengran: You, me, your Uncle Krik and Tully. Who else?

Ia: Oh, brilliant, Greengran.

~

Which brought them around the pond and three-quarters of the way up the avenue. The rowdy crows were quieter, dozily gossiping, comfy in their untidy nests.

'Go on indoors, Ia,' said Greengran, 'I need a quick word with Douglas Bethehokey. It's just possible Daffodil may calve tonight.' She sighed. 'Back to work.'

The evening moon lay on its back, banana fashion. Was it new or old that way up? Ia never knew. Anyway, there was no money in Muna's old coat to turn over for a new moon wish. She smiled inside, feeling more sister than daughter to Muna, the schoolgirl owner of this coat. New or old, the moon was beautiful and sailed like a canoe in and out of the soft scuffs of cloud; its light, and that scattered by the earliest stars of evening, filtered through the trees on either side of the short, wide avenue. An intensity of loneliness struck Ia to a sudden halt, a condition strange to her, unexpected, one she did not like. She felt shaken, and trod forward to the lighted windows of the house on heavy feet.

Tully bounded through the doorway. 'You OK?' he asked, skidding to a halt.

'Er ... yes. I really am tired, though.'

'I couldn't keep awake inside there and Krik's dozed off. I'm going to collapse into bed with a supply of writing paper. I want to try out an idea or two, but I'll probably fall asleep in the middle of it.' He paused. 'You're coming down to the lodge tomorrow, remember. Come in time for breakfast.'

'What will I get to eat?'

'Cornflakes, anyway!'

Ia's downcast moment had flashed away. An early bedtime was a good idea but not before a mental replay of the expedition to the Japanese Gardens, standing in front of the portrait in her bedroom.

'I did try,' she mumbled to it, half asleep.

Chapter 7

After the cornflakes, Tully fried slices of black and white puddings, rashers of smoked bacon, a couple of sausages, and an egg each.

'I don't go to Scouts for nothing,' he said, adding the final touch, white soda bread fried crisp and golden, 'and Teresa stocks me up. Coffee?'

'It smells gorgeous, Tully.' Ia felt as cosy as a cat in the warm kitchen-plus-everything room. She cleared her plate as if no food had passed her lips for a month.

His mother's pictures and experimental patterns glowed in richly coloured swirls and sworls against the matt white walls, all signed *Cliona Carrigaline*. His father's pottery, plates, platters, bowls and mugs, glazed in a variety of deep cobalt blues, bottle greens, apricot yellows, crimsons and burning browns, balanced on the shelves of the black-oak dresser, or dangled from its cup hooks. Built-in cupboards filled every nook and niche. The small latticed window sill shone glossy ember-red. Knobs, handles and cupboard edges glistened black, and black velvet curtains framed the small window. A circular jute mat on the floor pleased the eye.

Tully buttered his own toast and pushed a honey pot towards Ia. 'From my bees.' A smile twitched at the corner of his lips.

'Coo-*er*, you all *do* things, don't you?' Ia felt useless.

'Well, Da and Ma aim to be fairly self-supporting; we use everything that's around us, clay for Da's pots, and plants for dyes and paints ...'

'I don't do *anything*.'

'There's plenty inside you,' Tully said, 'it just hasn't surfaced yet.' He gave her a straight look, then checked his watch. 'D'ye know, it's still only five minutes to eight. It's lucky I was awake when you arrived. Do you want to have a look at the rest of the place? It's pretty small, so it won't take long.'

Tully kept his bedroom to the last. Theatre programmes and photographs of famous actors covered the walls. His iron-framed, double bunk had rainbow-shaded covers which echoed the window curtains and, on the opposite wall, a ten foot long plank-shelf hung suspended by ropes from two ceiling hooks and on it slept an outgrown family of bears — Teddy, Sooty, Rupert, Yogi — and a shabby elephant leaning against a hundred or so books, a pocket transistor radio, a huge pile of writing paper, and an old, glass sweet-jar crammed with pencils, felt-tip pens and biros. The windowsill, sapphire blue, marked out the two-foot deep lodge walls. The rest, a small low table, a wardrobe and an old electric storage heater, were as brightly painted as the windowsill. Level with the top bunk in which Tully slept (the rumpled duvet was the clue), shone a stained-glass window the size of a photograph album. A mini-reading lamp stood on the mini-windowsill.

'*Brilliant*,' breathed Ia.

'You've pinched my word again.'

'Sorry. I never noticed.'

'Oh, well, if it's not on purpose, I suppose it's all right. Come on, I'll show you Mam's studio and Dad's pottery shed.'

He lifted the latch of the back door. Red brick walls enclosed a small garden packed with flowers, fruit, vegetables ... and bees. Ia jerked away from the hives.

'If you leave them alone, they'll leave you alone. They're only waking up properly now after the winter.' Tully scooped up a handful of bees. 'Watch!' The bees crawled to and fro on his palm as if drunk.

'Er, can we go now?'

'Sure. You'll get used to them.'

'Hm,' said Ia.

He opened the door of a glasshouse attached to one wall. 'Mam's studio,' he said, 'it's always warm as toast inside. She can't work if it's cold.'

Ia saw easels, palettes, paint pots, brushes of every size, wall-hangings, embroidery threads in a cascade of colours, delicate silky materials, needles shining in a blue velvet pin cushion.

'Of course she has taken her super-super designs to the States,' said Tully, 'so the ones in the kitchen are all you can see for now; ditto Da's best stuff.'

'How do you *get* to have such brilliant, er, I mean

fabulous parents?'

'What's wrong with yours — Cordon Bleu Ma, Aircraft Designer Da?'

'Was.'

'OK. Aircraft Designer was. Science Fiction writer *is*. Coo-er! That's what *you* say. Here's the pottery shed, it's always a mess — the kiln there is for baking the pots, and this is his potter's wheel. It's more interesting when Da is throwing pots.'

'*Throwing* them?'

'Making, that's throwing.' Tully sat on the rough wooden bench. 'We haven't said anything about yesterday, have we? What do you think?'

'Well ...' Ia hesitated, 'I went to sleep like a stone the second I got into bed last night, then I bounced out this morning and down here so fast I haven't thought anything much. I had to creep through Greengran's room — she was still dead to the world — but I did tell her last night about coming here for breakfast, so she won't mind.'

Ia knew she was withholding something essential whilst, at the same time, she needed the comfort of sharing it. How could she explain anything so wispy to him, to herself? Had she just imagined that sudden cliff of loneliness? But twice? On the same day?

Tully snapped his fingers, made her jump. 'You seem to make a habit of going off like that, daydreaming, or whatever.' Finding he was excluded from her thoughts annoyed him somehow.

'Well, Miss Porrage says I do.'

'Miss *who*?'

'Porrage, my history teacher. She has a face a bit like

a plastic sponge.'

'I bet she has with a name like that. Sounds like my worst one, Mr Beverage. Old Tea Leaves, we call him.'

'I do daydream sometimes, but not that much.'

'What much?'

'Oh, well, the Japanese Gardens got me going, I suppose. I had a funny feeling a couple of times in there.' She brushed pottery-clay crumbs from one side of the trestle table to the other and back again, over and over.

'Same here, as a matter of fact, especially the married bit.' Tully was twirling the potter's wheel. 'That felt very peculiar, I can tell you, but I can't seem to work any of it into a play. Writer's block, it's called, I think.' He leaned his head to one side, listening. 'Sh!' he said.

Now what? Ia wondered

'*Listen*.'

'I can't hear anything.'

'That's exactly it. The water ram has stopped!'

~

Tully yanked open the hall door just as Douglas Bethe-hokey raised his fist to strike it.

'Ha! Ye're ready, then, Bethehokey. Off with ye, me boyo.'

Tully snatched his hand-whittled club from the brass umbrella stand and adjusted its leather thong about his right wrist so that it swung like a pendulum. The club's lower half looked as if it had stirred a can of crimson paint. 'Meet Captain Blood,' said Tully.

'Don't be minding that fella,' said Douglas Bethehokey.

'Isn't the stick only for beating back the nittles from stinging himself?'

'Ia, will you open the door for Teresa when she comes? She'll be checking on me any minute now. Meet you up at the house in half an hour or so.' Tully fished out a second club, painted blue. 'You can borrow Bluebeard today, if you like.'

'Where are you *going*?' asked Ia.

'Ask Douglas.'

Douglas peered into the coffee percolator, then reached for a mug and filled it to the brim. Because Tully ran fastest, his job was to find whereabouts the stream had been dammed, he explained, then Mr Krik and himself would be off to fix it, along with herself and Tully, if they hadn't anything better to do, 'not like the grand day out they had to themselves yesterday with the O'Maras, and the donkeys, bethehokey. And are ye settling well into Garriphouca, then? Nothing strange at all to be bothering ye?'

Ia met his diamond-bright grey eyes. What did his last question mean? 'I love it here,' she replied, cagily.

'That's grand, that's grand now.' The door knocker rapped. 'That will be Teresa. Let her in, there's the good girl, while I finish off me drink.'

'Is that Douglas in there with ye? The ram's stopped!'

'Tully's gone,' said Ia.

'That will be all right, so. Didn't ye think it was a bit cold down the avenue just now, Douglas?' Teresa said, snatching up the frying pan and broken egg shells.

'I'll wash up with you, Teresa.' Fair is fair, thought Ia.

'It will only take a minute with the two of us.' Teresa turned on the hot water tap. 'Ye'll want to be off up the stream with the others, won't ye? Tell us, did ye have a grand day out yesterday?'

Ia dried the dishes, told of their donkey riding, getting lost, the nearly-accident with the racehorses, the Rathcur Grasslands and the picnic, anything and everything, but not the Japanese Gardens. But she needed to know something of Teresa, the girl. At last, she dared:

'Do *you* ever go that way?' she asked.

'Ah, sure, I'm too old for all that now.' Teresa swapped looks with Douglas.

'She just thinks that,' he muttered, jerking his cap down to eye level. 'Bethehokey, didn't the both of us walk our legs to the bone often enough that selfsame way?'

'That's a long time since.' Teresa looked out the window, her face red. 'And wasn't that only because we went searching there for ...' The door clicked shut behind Douglas, cutting her sentence in half.

'Er, why were you and Douglas searching, Teresa? What for? Was that a long time ago? Did you find whatever it was? I suppose it wasn't anywhere near the Japanese Gardens, was it?'

Teresa's swift turnabout stopped Ia's stream of questions short. Had she said too much? The chance had seemed too good to miss.

'*Who* told you about that?' snapped Teresa.

'Do you mean about my grandfather disappearing, and all that?'

Teresa's round face unwound, then grew taut again.

'Do ye know no one talks to *her* about that?'

'I know, I know, I've promised I won't, and neither will Tully.'

'Tully!' Outrage swelled Teresa's globular body. 'Ye've told him? That's a fine promise ye've kept, I don't think.'

'He knew, Teresa, he knew already, I didn't tell him, his own parents did, the day before they went away. I know it sounds funny but it's true. Honestly, Teresa.'

Teresa exhaled, deflating like a large balloon, her everyday smile sweeping back into each crinkle and crevice.

'That makes us four, then: me and Douglas, yerself and Tully, six with his Ma and Da, of course.'

'You mean that you and Douglas could tell us a bit more about Greengranpa?'

'Ah, sure, there's no more than you know, really. He's been gone since that day, that's for sure, leaving your Greengran neither fish, flesh, nor fowl, as they say, and she a beautiful woman with two little babbies ...'

'But you were *there*, Teresa, outside the Gardens with Greengran, having a picnic with her and the babies. What happened? What *happened*? No one has told us what happened *afterwards*.'

'There is a little bit to tell,' admitted Teresa, licking her lips as if they were too dry, 'but if ye're going with the others to fix up the stream, ye'd better be away with yourself.'

'When, then? *When* will you tell us?'

'I think I'll be down the village to Mrs Goodey's shop about half past two, to get Tully a couple of things. I'll see yiz both down there, and then we can go to me house for a cup of tea. Then I'll tell ye.'

'Is Douglas coming?'

'Ah, that fella's always a bit contrary, with his

bethehokey this and bethehokey that, and all the rest.
But ye can say to him about the cup of tea, if ye like.'

Teresa flapped the wet dishcloth straight with a snap
and slipped it over the Aga rail to dry. She walked to
the hallway with Ia. 'Be off with ye now,' she said.

'Oh, I nearly forgot Bluebeard.' Ia picked out Tully's
club from amongst the walking sticks and umbrellas. Its
grip felt smooth and comfortable to her hand.

~

Tully danced like a dervish at the top of the avenue,
whirling Captain Blood in wide sweeping signals.

'Come on!' he yelled.

Ia ran towards him but Bluebeard swung clumsily,
knocking splinters from her ankle bone, hindering
speedy progress. Tully diagnosed the fault at once.
'Hold it like this,' he said, demonstrating how the crown
of Captain Blood's 'head' nestled inside the palm of his
hand, his fingers and thumb clasped loosely about the
rest, gripping and releasing it with each pendulum
swing, its thong taking the club's main weight.

'Now, come *on*. Uncle Krik and Douglas went up the
wood yonks ago.'

'Why is everyone in such a hurry? It has happened a
million times before, hasn't it?'

'Yes, but if it's not fixed at once, the ram won't restart,
Garriphouca's water tanks get air-blocked, Uncle Krik
nearly explodes, the water system goes haywire for
days, and Greengran breathes fire and brimstone in Mr
Clintlock's direction like any dragon.'

'But they had lunch together the day before yesterday...'

'So?' Tully's look was quizzical. 'Come *on*.' Ia came
on, puffing heavily. 'Can't you run faster?' he asked.
'There's two more fields after this, I suppose you
remember.'

By the end of the second field, Ia's breathing was less
ragged; after climbing the gate out of the third field and
into the wood, it steadied to a strong rhythm.

'That's better,' said Tully, halting at the stream's edge
to remove his trainer shoes and socks. 'We paddle up-
stream from here. It's quicker, so you'd better take yours
off too, and roll up your jeans, like this.'

Ia expected the stream to refresh her feet, not
refrigerate them. Her ankle bones ached and her feet
numbed to disappearing point.

'It'll be all right in a minute,' Tully said, urging on
Captain Blood's manoeuvres to preserve her bare legs,
hands and face from nettle stings and bramble barbs.
Her feet started coming back to life but that was because
the stream ran out of water.

'Oh, blow it, the basin's empty.'

'That little pool you showed me the other day?'

'That's the one. It feeds the stream and keeps things
going for a bit, long enough to avoid the air-block. At
least it does when we get here fast enough. Looks like
we're too late this time.'

'I hear something,' said Ia.

She heard a metallic thump and a tornado of vigorous
words in Douglas Bethehokey's voice, similar to the
volley of abuse poured over his 'dead' tractor yesterday.

'Ignore him,' chuckled Tully, 'we all do. He doesn't

even notice what he says.'

'There, man, you're not dead yet.' Uncle Krik's sympathy sounded edgy. 'Hand me the axe before you drop that as well.'

'They seem to have started! Douglas seems to have knocked a chunk out of himself. We'd better keep out of their way and just be on hand to fetch and carry whatever is needed.'

Ia trailed Tully across the pebbly floor of the dried-out pool and the last yard or two of the stream's bed to where the dam lay.

'Not much of a dam, really, just stones and tree trunks, sometimes a bit of cement, but it usually works OK.'

Uncle Krik jiggled a tree trunk loose with a grunt and pushed an iron lever between two heavy branches. Fine sweat bubbles pricked out on his nose. The whole area was messy and muddy, churned up by their feet. Douglas limped forward to add his weight to the lever. The branches rose, angled apart, toppled.

'Hand us the rope there, one of you.'

'Nice to be noticed, isn't it? whispered Tully, wryly.

He darted to the rope, tangled one end into a noose and tried to loop it around a notch, under a barrage of conflicting instruction from the two men.

'Now, everyone, *heave*,' said Uncle Krik.

The four of them lined the rope like a tug-of-war team, heels digging down, bodies lying back, exerting every atom of pulling power.

'Bethehokey, yiz aren't pulling at all. Come on. Try!' gasped Douglas.

'Shut up, Douglas,' panted Uncle Krik. 'Save all that

steam. *Heave.'*

The branch gave way without warning, cannoning their bodies into a heap, Uncle Krik being last man and a cushion for the others. In fifteen minutes, each was as mudsmeared as a New Guinea mud man, but the way was clear, the stream back on course, leaving a lesser tributary to trickle towards the mill. Uncle Krik wiped himself with bunches of grass.

'You'd better get the letter now, Tully,' he said, 'and take Ia with you. We'll head for the ram. Come on, Douglas.'

'Will do, Uncle Krik.' Tully dropped back into the stream.

'What letter is he talking about?' asked Ia.

'That's the next act.' Tully's raucous laugh rang out. 'While we work here, Greengran is writing a red-hot letter to Mr Clintlock, which has to be delivered by hand, *my* hand.'

'I see,' said Ia, not seeing.

Greengran's letter was ready, sealed inside a long, thin and elegant grey envelope. Her dangling earrings were skeletons.

~

Ia panted as they waited outside the mill gateway, the gate-porter telephoning through to the office, announcing their arrival.

'I didn't think Greengran was going to let me come, did you?' she said. 'I've never seen her look like that before.'

'Like what?' Tully's breathing was also rapid. The

downhill gradient of Garriphouca's village street forced legs to run faster than nature intended.

The inset portion of the admission gate clicked open. The gate porter looked knowingly at the grey envelope. 'That will be throwing fat on the fire,' he said. 'You know the way.'

'Did you tell him there's two of us today?' asked Tully.

'Never thought of it.' The man gave Ia a curious glance. 'The granddaughter, is it? Sure, that will be a grand surprise for himself ... well,' he added, rethinking, 'maybe, it will.'

'Not too encouraging, is he?' Tully grabbed Ia's hand. 'Come on. This way.' He pushed open the main building's black swing door. 'Up the stairs.' Clacking and clanking machinery reverberated the body of the mill. 'That means the water-wheel's still turning, thank goodness, because everything is as quiet as the grave if that's out of action, except for Mr Clintlock of course.'

A door snapped back on the floor above. Short, sharp footsteps rapped across bare wood. A burly, bullet-headed figure, arms akimbo, legs astraddle, stood at the stair top, waiting, watching ... Ia.

Tully brandished the grey envelope. 'Letter for you, Mr Clintlock.'

'I'd never guess from whom, I suppose?'

'You just might be able to, sir.'

'Come on up. I won't eat you. Aren't you supposed to put it into my hand?' The slim grey envelope changed hands.

It's like a chess game with set moves, thought Ia. Mr Clintlock had not once removed his eyes from her, unmatched eyes, one light brown, one blue. She found this combination as fascinating as the tilt and lilt of his voice.

'Come on up to my office, little Ia. I'd like to take a closer look at Sophia Fairley's granddaughter.'

Ia found this remark unsettling: I'd forgotten about Greengran being Sophia, she thought, although that's why I'm Ia, after all, but it's peculiar hearing someone talk about Greengran like that, Sophia Fairley, as if she's a person *he* knows, and I don't. She watched him prop the letter against a leather-framed photograph on his desk.

'I'll read that later,' he murmured, opening a drawer and taking out a sheet of notepaper. He scribbled on it, folded the note into three, tucked it inside an envelope, licked the gum and smoothed down the flap. He wrote *Sophia Fairley* on the envelope, handed it to Ia. 'There,' he said. 'I have to keep the water-wheel turning, you know. Business is business.' He tipped her chin up with a stubby finger. His bullet head nodded. 'Yes, he's there all right.'

'Did *you* know him, then?' Ia dared greatly. She was gambling on the identity of that 'him'.

'Your grandfather? Oh, yes, I knew him, but I knew Sophia first. Sophia Ringaskiddy, she was then. But what's the use of talking about it? The way she is now is the way she is, full stop. She has a blank space right inside, which all that liveliness of hers keeps well covered and locked from us all, herself included.' He sighed, as absent from them as if he had left the room.

The lightning glance Ia received from Tully told Ia he was seeing Mr Clintlock in a new light. He had slipped out his notebook for a quick squiggle or two. Ia broke the silence.

'I'd love to see your water-wheel,' she said.

'You would?' Mr Clintlock sprang up, grasped her hand, heading for the stairs. 'That's the girl,' he grinned.

Round and plain his face might be, thought Ia, long-spacing her legs to suit his, but when it lights up like that it is sort of er, um, satisfactory.

Tully jerked her elbow. 'You're cunning,' he whispered, 'I've been here a million times and never seen the water-wheel.'

Joy and pride oozed from Mr Clintlock's every pore. The water-wheel *was* beautiful. The dazzling orange paintwork of the wheel's outer rim and the emerald green of its spokes, six feet from hub to rim, if an inch, glittered in the water as cubes and prisms of light. Its slow revolutions splashed its paddles into and out of a waist-high circle of water cradled inside a wall of grey granite. Sparkling droplets hung in the air. Gentle creaks and splashings lingered in the ear. Silence united the three for a long moment, contentment curling inside each like a purring cat.

'But *how*,' Ia said, at last, 'how *can* Greengran not like it?'

'She has never seen it.'

'Never *seen* it?'

'She won't come.'

'Obstinate, that's what,' muttered Tully, under his breath.

'Not exactly, although maybe a bit.' Mr Clintlock's tuneful voice rose and fell. 'When she was a young girl she had no interest in such things, and then afterwards

... well, then our battle started. I am not sure at all how it did, it's so long ago, or who started it but now the stream is a little weapon of sorts.' A small, bleak smile came and went. 'But never mind about that now, it's time you were on your way. Do I take it the ram needs restarting?' Tully nodded. 'Then there will be no peace until that's done. It's an accident when my men stop the ram, young Ia, but I must have enough water to turn the wheel.' He held his hand out to her. She shook it.

Chapter 8

'He never shakes *my* hand,' said Tully.

'I'm new,' said Ia.

'You're also Greengran's granddaughter, I'd say.'

'Mm, could be. Oh, Tully,' her memory jerked, 'I forgot to tell you something.'

'What?'

'Teresa *knows*.'

'What does she know?'

'Knows *we* know.'

'Knows we know what?'

'The deep, dark mystery of missing Granpa, that's what.'

'Coo-er, as you say. Explain.'

She did, clearly, and about Teresa's hint of another clue or two to go with a cup of tea.

'There's not too much time, then, it's nearly one o'clock now. And I don't hear the ram yet so they must still be working on it. Come on.'

I wonder how many times he has said 'come on' today, thought Ia. She also thought that climbing back up Garriphouca Hill was hard on her empty stomach.

'I'm hungry,' she complained.

'We'll get something from the fridge after.'

'After what? And I haven't told Mr Bethehokey that he is invited.'

'Tell him in a minute, only don't let Uncle Krik hear you.'

They ran past the house to the kitchen garden, sloping down to the stream's edge from the west turret. Surrounded by rows of cauliflowers, cabbages, spinach, celery, carrots, potatoes, and a lot more, stood the ram. The squat little iron pump had a cast-iron personality and will of its own; whenever disturbed from normal routine, it resisted every effort to re-establish another with might and main; spanners and screws littered the ground and venomous words swarmed in the air like angry wasps as Uncle Krik probed the ram's intestines. Even Douglas Bethehokey looked shocked.

'It's the only time Uncle Krik really lets fly,' said Tully, 'he doesn't like being beaten by anything mechanical.'

The way Douglas stood by, handing tools over on demand, reminded Ia of hospital movies she had seen on TV about life-and-death operations when the surgeon has to have scalpels and forceps put into his hand at exactly the right moment. Douglas looked nervous.

'It's been over an hour this time,' he whispered behind Uncle Krik's back. 'Bethehokey, I'd give it a good kick myself.'

'Chisel!' snapped Uncle Krik.

'One chisel,' said Douglas. Ia leaned forward and whispered in his ear. 'A cup of tea with Teresa?' he gasped. His tools clinked to the ground.

Uncle Krik scowled, saw Ia and Tully and strove to control his verbal volleys.

'Pick them up, man, pick them up,' he growled to Douglas. 'Pass me that file. Not that one, the big one, you eejit.'

'One file.'

Uncle Krik grew more oily, sweaty, dirty. And weary. He dried his forehead and face with a rusty rag and sat on the ram's lidless edge, wiping his hands, drooping.

'I give up,' he muttered, 'this time, I really do give up.'

The ram surrendered at the selfsame moment, belching forth shattering thumps and chugs from its belly, shocking Uncle Krik to his depths, and to his feet in a stumble of rage to slam the ram's lid back on, barely avoiding its last vicious attempt to amputate his finger ends. Tears of mirth cascaded down Douglas and Tully's cheeks.

'It's always the same,' choked Tully, seeing Uncle Krik deal the stumpy water-worker an irritable kick, almost breaking his toe in the process.

'Bethehokey, does the man niver learn?'

'You know he never does, Douglas.' Tully nursed his stomach as he watched gusts of laughter overwhelm Ia. 'Don't let him see you,' he gasped. Still doubled up, he started running.

Ia ran after him in convulsive gambols but Uncle Krik was too involved in his one-footed dance of pain to notice.

~

Their names came keening through the air, thin, high.

'Ia-a-a-a! Tull-eee!'

Ia stopped dead, astounded. 'That can't be *Green-gran.*'

'That's her. It's even better, or worse,' he grinned, 'when she wants someone in the Top Field.'

'Tull-ee-ee-ee! Ia-aa-aa-aa!'

'She's revving up,' said Tully.

'Coo-er.' Greengran's soft voice, transformed to a shrill siren call, amazed Ia.

'Watch out. The next one will split your eardrums.'

'Let's get back before she does, then.'

They avoided Greengran's sound-barrier crash-through by a breath.

'Ah, there you are. Good.' Greengran, the sophisticated city lady, stood beside her Mini in front of the house, tailored and trim in smooth, mink-shaded jacket, skirt and supple suede court shoes, utterly composed, giving no indication of anything unusual. 'I just thought I'd better have Mr Clintlock's reply to my letter before leaving.' She checked the fastening of her left earring, a tiny golden horseshoe. 'For luck,' she said, flicking it into a swing with a fingernail. She did not remark on the creased condition of Mr Clintlock's note, merely tucking it into the paper money section of her black leather executive wallet.

'Is that *all* you wanted, Greengran?'

'That's all, Ia. Oh, except I've decided it's the day after tomorrow for Poolgorum, so don't plan anything else, will you? This afternoon I'm seeing my solicitor, so we'll talk about everything later this evening. We'll take the pony and trap, by the way ... Jenny needs the exercise.'

'Am *I* coming?' Tully asked.

'I expect Ia would have something to say if you didn't, Tully. Right, Ia?'

'Right, Greengran.'

Tully liked the way the two moved close together, as if that was important. It warmed him. He mentally photographed them standing so, in front of the ivy-clad house, knowing he could switch the picture back any time he liked.

'Haven't you two eaten yet?'

'We're just going to,' Ia said.

'There's a few pork pie slices, and tomatoes. How about that?'

Greengran slid into the once-white Mini's driving seat. The car pranced like a racehorse from the starting post, rear wheels crunching aside the gravel, swinging into the avenue, raising dust into the air. Yellow sunshine shafted through the tree trunks, striking spangles and sparks from the car's windows, twisting the eyes, or so Ia fancied, blinking them first, then staring them wide open for a long, impossible moment.

She was not seeing things. No, she was not. *Greengran's Ghost Lady*. Who else? In her long dress, plain as anything, something fan-shaped in one hand, wafting it, beckoning with it ... Ia felt icy cold, turned to Tully. He was halfway through the hall door, looking back at her.

'Come on,' he shouted, 'I thought you were hungry.'

'I, er, yes, I'm coming,' she called, her eyes shooting back to the avenue. Nothing there. *Nobody*. Oh, goodness,

I hope I'm not going funny. Maybe my eyes are. I might need glasses. It must be the way the light and shade criss-crosses through tree trunks and pergolas that does it ... but ... but Greengranpa did *paint* the Ghost Lady, even if he pretended to Greengran that it was only a joke.

Muna's voice echoed once again in Ia's ears, every syllable: 'Douglas told me my father saw the Ghost Lady quite regularly, that she was like a friend to him, and no harm to anyone at all.'

No harm to anyone at all. The phrase balanced Ia. She knuckled her eyes. Again, nothing. Nobody. It could be something to do with, what's it called? Oh, yes, I know, ESP ... like that Uri Geller man who bends forks and spoons just by *thinking*. Extra-sensory perception, that's what that is. Maybe that's what I have. She pursed her lips, vaguely pleased, vaguely alarmed. Do I tell Tully, though?

'You've taken your time,' said Tully.

It was an effort to smile, but Ia did it. He can think what he likes, she thought, a slice of pie in one hand, a tomato in the other. I'll wait until we've had tea in Teresa's before deciding whether to tell him or not.

'Put your skates on,' said Tully, his own ESP reaching into a part of her mind. 'We don't need to drink now if Teresa is going to give us a cup of tea. It's time to go, and we still haven't said what we really think about the Japanese Gardens.'

Teresa was inside Mrs Goodey's shop when they arrived. They saw her through the window, beyond the giant white cat stretched behind the window pane, ice-blue eyes disdainful; the window was a jumble of dummy candy cartons, faded rubber balls, capsized plastic toys, out-of-date Christmas annuals and shining baubles for bygone Christmas trees. Entering the shop was to step back into time, the ceiling's wooden beams a dangle of dustpans, brooms, clothes-horses, garden canes, mouse and rat traps, toddlers' tricycles, kettles, toy drums and skipping ropes. Ia's nose exploded into sneezes as the variety of odours (a build-up of many years trading) tickled her nostrils. She swivelled, tracing them to their sources: small, home-made lavender bags, onions shedding their skins, a duster trapped in a half-open tin of beeswax polish, a demijohn of brown vinegar, a drum of paraffin, a baker's wooden tray of crusty bread; open sacks on the plain wooden floor displayed chicken meal, dog biscuits and pigeon pellets; slatted boxes spilled out lemons, oranges and bananas. An ageless, unhurried air blended the potpourri of aromas.

Tully pinned his gaze to the glass sweet jars on the shelf behind Mrs Goodey's head, unaware that the shop was in the least unusual. Teresa's ballooning bosom leaned on the counter, punctuating each purchase from Mrs Goodey by soft whispers and side glances towards Ia. Mrs Goodey was so small, slow moving and old that Ia wondered how she managed to shop-keep at all, yet she was surprisingly spry. She used a lightweight, mobile platform arrangement as an assistant. It slid along behind the counter length at the touch of a finger and it had a lever which raised a platform step up and down the shelves. Mrs Goodey allowed her customers (Teresa anyway) to serve themselves from the shelves and boxes in the well of the shop, piling their choices on to the counter for Mrs Goodey to weigh, price and drop into their shopping baskets, only now and then using a paper bag.

'And some of these, Mrs Goodey,' said Teresa, lifting the glass-lidded biscuit tins, inviting Ia and Tully to pick and choose their favourites. 'I have visitors this afternoon, Mrs Goodey,' she said, with a wink.

Mrs Goodey twisted up a couple of paper cones and secretly filled them up as Tully and Ia biscuit browsed.

'There,' she said, scooping a strand of snow-white hair from her wrinkled forehead, 'they're the same as your mammy used to buy with her pocket money, every Saturday, regular as clockwork. One for each of ye. Just a little present.'

'Oh, *thank you*, Mrs Goodey,' said Ia, astonished.

Tully nudged her. 'Look inside — Peggy's Leg, Bulls' Eyes, Love Hearts, Acid Drops, a liquorice bell-push, a pipe and two bootlaces.'

Ia turned at the door. 'I'll come and spend *my* pocket money next Saturday,' she said.

'Get along with the both of ye, now,' Mrs Goodey's filmy-brown eyes shone like chestnut conkers for a moment. 'Don't be keeping Teresa waiting.'

Teresa sent Tully to the lodge with the shopping, except for the biscuits, and puffed uphill with Ia to her own cottage, sixth in a row of twelve, staring across fields to a tall church spire.

'Do you live by yourself, Teresa?'

'That I do.' Teresa lifted the door latch.

'Don't you lock the door when you go out?'

'That I don't. Sure, we all know each other round here, it's safe enough, not like down in the city. Come in to my doll's house. Tully won't be a minute. We'll leave the door ajar for himself and Douglas.'

Ia envied Tully his gate lodge but this, this ... well, it is so *little*, and perfect with its white-white walls, and shining black-black woodwork, bright-bright scarlet curtains, carpets and mats; a sitting room with twenty-three shining brass kettles, a bedroom, a kitchen, a bathroom. A sun porch at the back led into ... Ia swayed, dumbfounded ... *a miniature Japanese Garden*. Teresa's hands steadied her.

'There now,' she said, 'that's my little secret. No one knows anything about it, except that Douglas, of course — he built those high walls all round as well as making the Garden — oh, and Tully's Mammy knows, too.'

A breath hissed behind them. 'Brilliant!' said Tully.

'Doesn't Muna know?' asked Ia.

'Not her either. She might have let it slip over the years, without meaning to, of course.'

'What about me letting it slip?' said Ia.

Teresa appeared surprised. 'There's something about ye, people are saying, people that remember your granpa — like Johnjoe, Douglas, Mrs Goodey — well, they're saying that ....'

'You mean they all think I look a bit like *him*?' asked Ia. How could she be like that golden-bearded man in her bedroom?

'It's the way ye gaze around ye, turn your head, that sort of thing, a kind of *looking* look he had.'

'And the way she stands about, bethehokey, as if she's waiting for someone. I've seen her at that a couple of times already, the same way he'd be ...' Douglas halted, seeing Teresa's eyes examining his feet.

'Did ye wipe those boots?' she asked.

'I did, Teresa, I did.'

'All right, then. Stop standing half-in, half-out of the door and show them the Garden while I wet the tea.'

~

The Garden area was hardly twelve yards long, ten wide. A higgledy-piggledy cobble-stoned pathway ribboned up and down and in and out, skirting a flat centre of smooth pebbles, raked into perfect scrolls and whorls; an occasional, set-in rock emphasised the pattern's perfection. A knee-high facsimile Tea House stood on the 'hill' overlooking a pool of goldfish; on its banks, a fat, blue buddha figurine sat crosslegged, affably smiling, and a model of the Japanese Gardens' scarlet bridge spanned the pond's water. Miniature stone lanterns (cast in cement here) 'lit' the shrubs and curly-trunked small trees, almost like bonsai but not quite, which were awash with blossoms of scarlet, cream, pink and gold. Ia and Tully had nothing to say.

'D'ye not like it at all?' asked Douglas in scandalised tones.

'Yes, but, well, I ...' said Ia.

'Well, isn't it the divil and all? All my life, and Teresa never showed it to me. She never *told* me.' Indignation pushed loud cracks into Tully's voice.

'Why is she telling yiz now, then? Bethehokey, I don't know that myself. Ye have to wait a long day for that one to tell ye her mind, that I know full well.'

'It's unbel*iev*able,' said Ia, still mesmerised, 'it's so, so, out of this *world*. Teresa.'

'Of course, I know that. Sit down on that rocking chair, Tully. That's your Mammy's favourite.'

'Is it?' He tested its rocking power, thoughtfully.

'And Ia here beside me.' Teresa patted a pretty three-legged chair with a semi-circular back. 'Douglas knows his own place.'

'I used to,' Douglas muttered. His leathery cheeks flared dark red.

'Take off that cap, then, ye used to do that as well, didn't ye?'

'Teresa,' he said, the flat cap rotating slowly between his fingers, the beginnings of a smile at his lips, 'are we going to ...?'

'Give me that cap and there's your own tea cup. The sugar is looking at ye. I suppose you'll empty the bowl, *as usual.*'

Even as Teresa was interrupting Douglas, she met and matched his smile before hanging the cap on a hook at the back of the door. He tipped three mountainous spoons of sugar into the large cup.

'*As usual,*' he said.

Tully shot Ia a questioning glance during this exchange. She shook her head, shrugged her shoulders and raised her eyebrows, seized by mystification. She let her brain go limp and sipped tea from a delicate green china cup, fragile as an eggshell, on its lip a hairline border of gold.

'Japanese,' said Teresa, smugly. 'These cups are only for us ladies; they'd be broke in a minute with them two.'

'Wherever did you get them?' asked Ia.

'Sure, someone gave them to me once.'

Douglas shifted in his chair. 'Now, Teresa,' he began, uneasily.

'Now nothing,' said Teresa, 'they know all about the Japanese Gardens and him vanishing the way he did, and if ye hadn't been so quick out of the door this morning, ye would have heard Ia tell that. That's where they went yesterday. The Japanese Gardens, no less, trying to ferret out a bit more for themselves. So, then, I thought, well, maybe we'd better tell them what they want, if they swear Cross their Hearts and Hope to Die, niver to let Mrs Greengran hear a thing about it.' Teresa's shelf-like bosom steadied.

'Bethehokey,' said Douglas, 'so that's why I am darkening your door again, is it?'

'It's half the why, anyway.'

The little room went mute, except for the creak of the rocking chair, and cup to saucer clinking. By craning her neck, Ia could see part of the magical Garden through the window. At least *it* did not disappear when she looked away. But why did Teresa have a Japanese Garden? Why did she keep it secret?

'Eat up those biscuits with your tea. Pass the plate to Ia, Tully.'

Crunching. Another sigh from Teresa. Douglas went Hm! Hm! clearing his throat.

'What did ye think to find out?' he asked Tully and Ia. 'What do ye want to know? Did ye discover anything at all? What did ye think of the Gardens there?'

'You're nearly as bad as Ia with all the questions,' smiled Tully, and told the facts, how they hoped to demystify the mystery of Ia's missing grandfather, as well as giving him, Tully, a brilliant plot for the play he was writing, well, going to write, next week probably. 'We still don't know why he got amnesia, or whatever, but the Gardens were brilliant, weren't they, Ia? We felt sort of er, em, er ...'

'Deep.' Ia chose the word. 'We felt *deep*, about ourselves, each other really, and about Greengran and Greengranpa being young and married, things like that; then, as well, I'm not sure how to explain it ...'

'They do say those Gardens are supposed to make people think a lot,' said Teresa.

Ia inhaled, steeling herself. Her face whitened. She grabbed at courage. 'Mr Bethehokey,' she said, 'down the avenue ... Greengran's Ghost Lady ...' Douglas and Teresa stiffened to attention, '... he often saw her, didn't he? My mother said you told her that he did and that the Ghost Lady was like a friend to him. Well, I mean, how did you *know*? Did Greengranpa tell you? Did *you* see her? *Is she still in the avenue*?'

Tully's chair ceased rocking.

'Ye see,' Teresa nodded at Douglas, 'it's one question after the other.'

'I thought it was the Japanese Gardens yiz wanted to ask about.' Douglas threw Teresa a sour glance.

'We do, we do,' said Ia, 'but we, *I* (her eyes flicked towards Tully) had this sort of feeling in the Japanese Gardens yesterday, *and*, as well, in the avenue last night, I thought I saw, well, *someone* who looked like the Ghost Lady in our oil painting at home.'

'Ah, the picture. Bethehokey, I did forget ye had that picture of his. Hm,' said Douglas. He studied Ia as if reading small print. 'Yes,' he said, finally, 'it's in ye the same as it was in him, so I'll answer ye the best I can.

Didn't your granpa and myself grow up alongside each other in this place, and when we had grown up and he got to be boss of Garriphouca House, wasn't I his right-hand man? Man to man, we'd talk, day in, day out, so, as soon as his Ghost Lady started visiting, he told me about her. All of a sudden he would stop dead on the avenue, like I saw ye doing only last evening, and he'd say: "Here she is again, Douglas. She's beckoning to me. Look! There she is." He'd say she was misty, shadowy, and she was wearing a long gown of some sort, what did he call it? a French-like kind of word ...'

'Neglijay, I think,' said Teresa.

'Well, that, and she would be cooling herself with a little fan. Bethehokey, I niver thought, would it be that fan of hers that makes the avenue go all cold after she's been?'

'Gosh,' said Tully.

'That fan might do it,' agreed Teresa.

Ia bit her lip. It hurt.

'And,' continued Douglas, emptying his cup in one gulp, clanging it back to its saucer, 'he would say the Ghost Lady was crying sometimes. He wanted to help her, but, sure, he didn't know how. A couple of years it went on like that. He didn't know whether to be telling your granma, or not. She might laugh at him, he'd say.'

'He was that good-looking a man, she'd be a bit jealous in those times,' nodded Teresa.

'So he painted her into his picture of Garriphouca House to see how Greengran would react, I suppose,' said Tully, 'but it didn't work, did it? We know that all right.'

'Do you think she kept on coming all these years and

no one saw her, until ...' Ia's voice faded.

'That's the funny thing ...' began Teresa, but Douglas interrupted for once.

'Teresa means we had forgotten her entirely, until just a few evenings since when I was walking home, and there was that cold patch under the trees, just like all that time ago.'

'I see,' said Ia. Her mind felt pulled to the bedroom portrait as if by an umbilical cord.

'There's no harm in the Ghost Lady at all,' said Douglas, 'I'm just wondering why she has come back.'

'Poor lonely lady,' sighed Teresa.

Tully made a discovery: 'You're like a TV receiver, Ia, that's what. You can pluck pictures out of thin air, *and so could your granpa.*'

'Something of that sort.' Douglas did not let on that Tully's reasoning impressed him.

'And there's ESP,' said Ia, slowly.

'There's *what*?' asked Teresa.

Ia explained how Uri Geller bent spoons and forks by thought alone: Douglas and Tully sidetracked enthusiastically into similar TV programmes they had seen.

'A ghost is a ghost, that's all,' said Teresa. 'Some people only *feel* them, like it being cold and that, and other people *see* them. Didn't ye say something about feeling the same way in the Japanese Gardens, Ia?'

'Well, sort of the same, only different, and ...' Ia's body rocked with the strength of her snap decision ... '*I have to go back.*'

'The same thing,' muttered Teresa. 'he had to do that, too, that's what I think.'

'So do I.' Ia turned towards Teresa. 'And he wanted

to go back by himself, like I do, to be on his own, and *quiet*, so that he could try and understand. Leaving the leaflet behind was an excuse. He probably thought Greengran would tease him, or laugh, if he told her his real reason.'

'The two of us did laugh and we enjoyed ourselves feeding the babbies and eating up the chicken and salad,' Teresa admitted, 'and then it seemed to be a long time so we went to the gate to call after him, but he didn't come. She started worrying, then, we asked the man at the gate to watch over the babbies in the pram while the two of us went in to find him. By this time, didn't we think he'd fallen down some place — he could be lying half dead, unconscious. We went every-which-way there was to go, and not a sign of him. Well, that was just the start.'

'He might have gone through the Gate of Eternity,' said Tully.

'That Eternity Garden wasn't made until a year afterwards,' said Douglas.

'The kiosk man said the walls were too high for anybody to climb over. There was only the one way out, beside his kiosk. We must have missed some of the paths, he said, so in he went to look for himself. 'I'll find him for ye,' he said, but he didn't. Ye should have seen his face! Then the owners of the Japanese Gardens came, and then the police, and those dogs that smell things and ...' Teresa was babbling.

'Bloodhounds,' said Douglas. 'Inside and outside the Gardens they were, sniffing and snuffing ...'

'For miles around ...' said Teresa.

'As far as the Rathcur grasslands,' explained Douglas.

'For weeks and weeks ...' said Teresa.

'Is that when you both did all the walking?' asked Ia.

'That's right,' said Douglas, 'but niver a thing did any one of us find.'

'Only the new babby,' said Teresa, lost in a reminiscent haze, 'but, of course, that was a good while after.'

Ia stared at her. 'What do you mean, a new baby?'

'Oh!' Teresa clapped a hand to her lips.

'Where was this baby, anyway?' Tully sounded impatient, thinking they had strayed a great deal too far from the main subject.

'Ye've let it drop now, my girl,' said Douglas, 'ye might as well get on with the rest of it.'

~

An hour later, Ia and Tully found themselves sitting on the raft inside its bamboo hideaway; they had stumbled there automatically, to be alone, to think.

'My head is still tied up inside,' muttered Tully.

Ia nodded, wandering in the labyrinth of Teresa's revelations. All right, she thought, sometimes newspapers do report babies found in funny places, like church doorways, and you think — What a shame! — but you forget it next minute. You don't really feel sorry about it having to grow up in a children's home. Just imagine being the one to find the baby, though. Of course, it had made the headlines in all the newspapers, the second Japanese Gardens mystery in one year; first, Greengranpa disappearing, and then this baby appearing from nowhere, at least nowhere anyone could find out about. Everyone appealed to the mother to come forward, but did she? She did not. So, although the baby was taken into care, it stayed crying in Teresa's mind, and no wonder. Finding it like that, actually *meeting* it, and then no one wanting it. Talk about complicated. Then Teresa's sister died (the one who worked in London) and that made up her mind somehow. She decided *she* would adopt the baby. Would it be possible? she asked Greengran.

At first Greengran didn't want to talk about it because that is how she was after Greengranpa disappeared and, anyway, she didn't think Teresa could, not being married. So what did Teresa do? She persuaded Douglas to London for a 'paper' wedding, so that, as a 'married woman', she could adopt the baby. 'But we weren't really married, only on that bit of paper,' said Teresa, 'of course, we were ever so young then.' She and Greengran kept the adoption secret. Indeed Teresa told outright lies in the village. It was her dead sister's baby, she told them. 'She wouldn't have minded, I know that,' said Teresa.

She brought up the little girl with no help from anyone, apart from Greengran's secret gifts of butter, eggs, milk, vegetables and fruit from the farm, 'On top of me wages for cooking up at the House.' The miniature Japanese Gardens idea only came into her head later. 'A way of thanking God for the gift-child he sent me,' said Teresa, all of a smile. 'Douglas and meself had the grand time getting it just right for the little one to play in.'

Tully lifted his baffled head, half surprised he was still sitting on the raft. 'It's funny I never heard of Teresa having a child before today,' he said.

'Well, Teresa did say the baby had grown up and

married before you were born, remember,' said Ia.

'Even so, you would think I'd have *heard* of her; you'd think my own mother might have mentioned it to me except, I suppose, Teresa told her not to tell me.'

'What I want to know is why it was OK for *your* mother to know, but not *mine*,' said Ia, indignantly. 'I wonder if they used to play together when they were small?'

'They're bound to have gone to the village school when they were little but, then, your mother and Uncle Krik went to a school in the city later on, I think, so maybe they didn't meet much, or at all.'

'I bet the O'Maras know. They seem to know things you don't, but we *do* know that *anything* about the Japanese Gardens is just not talked about round here, don't we?'

'Hm.'

A pause.

'I don't think we had enough questions for Teresa and Douglas to answer,' said Tully.

His remark flashed inside Ia's mind like an electronic camera flash, forcing her mental focus to adjust: 'Which means the answer to Greengranpa's disappearance *is* in the Japanese Gardens, if we knew the right question,' she said.

'Is that what I mean? Oh. Well. I get it, I think. So?'

'So, you see, I do have to go back.'

'We do, you mean, but when, how? It took four of us last time.'

'Tomorrow. We're going to Poolgorum the day after, Greengran said, remember. We can take the donkeys again, can't we? (Tully moaned, slightly.) We know the way now, don't we? But,' she was adamant, 'I am going into the Gardens by myself.'

'All right, on condition we go to the Garden of Eternity afterwards, both of us, OK?'

'OK,' Ia smiled. 'We can just tell Greengran we want another day out with the donkeys, without saying where to, of course.'

Uncle Krik said they could catch Spalpeen and Spud themselves because his toe was too sore to go tramping across the fields. Greengran absentmindedly noted the children's picnic plan. She was busy thinking of her afternoon's visit to the solicitor, which had, she said in a smug manner, 'brought results', and Mr Clintlock would be coming this evening to discuss matters. Ia's forkful of Teresa's shepherd's pie halted halfway to her mouth at this news but neither Uncle Krik nor Tully showed any surprise.

'Just the usual carry-on,' Tully whispered. His elbow nudge jerked the food off her fork.

'Don't get too tired, though,' Greengran said, 'there's lots of work for us all at Poolgorum the day after tomorrow. I know I said we'd arrange all that tonight, but there you are, that's the way it is ...'

'She's not really connecting,' whispered Ia, feeling deceitful.

'Teresa will fix up some picnic food for you, won't you, Teresa?' said Uncle Krik, more himself now with shepherd's pie inside him.

Teresa slid a golden-topped queen of puddings on to the table; saliva spurted into Ia's mouth at the sight. How was Teresa able to produce fabulous food so fast? It had been four o'clock when they left her cottage.

'Come down to the kitchen after this,' she said to Tully and Ia, 'we'll talk about it, then.'

Teresa had guessed, of course. They stayed in the kitchen for some time, helping to wash the dishes and wrap up tomorrow's tasty items in silver foil.

'It's better for us to be out of the way when those two meet,' Teresa said, hearing Mr Clintlock's noisy arrival upstairs, as well as the subsequent rise and fall of irritable voices behind the drawing room's closed doors. Uncle Krik limped through the kitchen, aiming to spend a convalescent hour or two with his car skeletons. When it was time for Tully to set off down the avenue, quieter zz — zz voice tones indicated a simmering truce of some sort upstairs.

'Just you take care tomorrow, Ia,' said Teresa.

Ia yearned for bed. I don't know why I'm so tired, she thought. She undressed and washed her teeth, studiously avoiding any glance towards the portrait. She did not feel strong enough to cope with that, *and* tomorrow.

Chapter 9

Ia stood rock-still inside the Gate of Forgetfulness, her head emptied out, waiting: even her eyes felt washed, fresh. The fears she had carried in her stomach all the way from Garriphouca dropped away. The world outside the pale wood palisade faded. Except for birds softly flitting and fluting, and the water rippling, only silence walked there. Brilliant colours shone from blossoming trees and flowering shrubs, more vivid, more vibrant by the second. Slowly, slowly, she stepped along the pathways of life drawn by those long ago gardeners from far away. She let her mind be, did not chase after meaning, as they had done the other day. The stone seat waited for her at the base of the Hill of Ambition. Ia sat on it, knowing this was where she wished to be.

Slowly, slowly, happiness seeped inside her, radiating shafts of joy and wonder. *That* island with its pink and purple, clematis-wrapped pergola poles and

beflowered tree-trunk bridge, appeared to float on air
as well as water. From nowhere to somewhere, a question sailed forth from Ia's mind like a small origami
boat, clear and concise: 'Tell me who you are, and how
you came here. First, you must look at me. Here I am.'

No shadow or water hallucination (nor Ghost Lady
either), Ia beheld a person as solid as herself, *a Japanese
person*, whose hair, black and shining as enamel paint,
was piled and shaped about her head and face like a
cottage loaf of bread, skewered here and there by stick-
like jewels. Jet-black eyebrows hovered like wings
above inky-dark almond eyes, emphasising the
porcelain-pale face. Her sharply defined mouth
reminded Ia of a small crimson butterfly. Over her
golden gown, dovetailing into a tiny train bordered in
bright blue, she wore a kimono of exotic patterning; tiny
feet in chalk-white socks balanced on raised wooden
sandals and an enormous blue sash tied above her waist
to secure a flat, cushiony affair against the small of her
back, its trailing ends fluttering when the lady wafted
the fan in her right hand, a fan veined and shaped like
an autumn-gold beach leaf.

'I am Su Su. You must not fear me,' she said.

'I'm not afraid of you, I'm just, just *mixed up*.' Ia heard
herself gasp.

'But you begin to understand that our thoughts speak
without voices?'

'Yes. Yes, I think I do. That's brilliant! I'm Ia.'

'This I know. But you wish to understand how I came
here? Chi Nu thought me.'

'Thought you? Oh, that can't be right, I don't think
I'm doing this properly.'

'It is strange for you to think-talk, that is all. Rest a moment.'

Su Su's teeth shone like mother-of-pearl behind the smiling crimson lips. Her strange beauty fascinated Ia.

'It is well now? I bring understanding to you?' The fan quivered.

Ia nodded, forgetting she did not need to.

'You know that gardeners came from Japan to create this garden and, to do so, they must remain here for several years?'

'Yes, I do know that.'

'One of those gardeners, Chi Nu, was my betrothed. Before our parting, we promised solemnly to meditate upon one another at a certain hour each day until he returned once again to Japan; to be so far apart was terrible to us, more terrible for Chi Nu in this cold and damp foreign land. Each sunset, he meditated one hour. *There*, where now you sit. His thoughts grew very strong until, at last, he was able to think me to him. It was strange, and very wonderful.' Su Su paused again, smiling, fanning.

'I can't wait, Su Su — go on!'

'Chi Nu called me his Thought-Wife. Every day I waited for his call but, each day, it became more difficult for him to wake from his meditation, to return me to my father's house. As the Gardens grew, and the plants and trees from Japan took root and became beautiful, so did our love, until ...'

Su Su lowered her head, moved the fan to cover her face. Ia felt Su Su's sadness wash into her.

'What is it? What happened? *Tell me*.'

'It rains so often in this land, not like Japan. Chi Nu

became ill. He called me to him, ceaselessly: he could not release me. He died in my arms, there, where now you sit.'

'Oh, Su Su.'

'His gardener friends came to seek him when the evening became too late. They hurried to a doctor and then — even though the doctor's thoughtwave was not mine — so great was my distress, I could read one of the words he thought ... pneumonia was that word.'

Ia half rose from the stone seat, offering comfort. Su Su's crimson lips and dark doe-shaped eyes smiled, receiving the offer.

'But once Chi Nu was dead ...?'

'I could not be his Thought-Wife? That is what you think, and that I must return to Japan? But did he not die in my arms? Was I not his Thought-Wife to that very last moment? He was too ill: he could not think me back to my father's house. I did not understand this for many days. I could feel the thoughts of my father and mother reaching out to me, thinking me dead, and I reached mine towards them, but we could not meet. Ia, only one or two, sometimes three, thoughtwaves can link lives together ... Chi Nu told me this. His and mine linked first, the second ...'

Ia picked up Su Su's thought so fast it stunned her.

'My grandfather!'

'This is correct, but there is a third also for me, Ia.'

'Ia felt calm, certain: 'I know ... it's *me*.'

At this revelation, Su Su's thought-said they both must rest awhile — she would walk to the waterfall and back. Then she would finish the story. Ia watched her step across the tree-trunk bridge, feeling loose-limbed and dreamy herself, unwinding. She closed her eyes until Su Su's silky kimono rustle signalled her return.

Thoughtwave telling the depths of her misery and loneliness upon realising she would be exiled alone, forever, plainly gave Su Su much pain. That intensity of loneliness had forced her to search desperately for a mind on her wavelength, following any likely signal to its source, however faint, until, one day, a strong line of thought led her to ...

'Garriphouca avenue,' flashed Ia. '*You* are the Ghost Lady?'

Su Su smiled, swiftly. 'To the man you call grandfather, but he could not see me clearly and he did not understand my need. Many times I signed him to follow me here, for communication is so simple in a garden of meditation. At last he came. I knew nothing of his earth-wife then, for it is only possible to see the person whose thoughtwaves are yours,' Su Su explained, a little sadly. 'Even then, it was difficult for us to thought-speak at first.'

'Was that because Greengran came in here with him?'

Su Su nodded: 'But then, when he returned to the Garden alone, it was as we are now, Ia, and, oh, it was wonderful for me. He promised to come and visit me often, and that we would try to find a way for his earth-wife also to see me, but then ...'

Ia's mind reeled round and round like an adrift television picture frame. Su Su's white hand reached towards her, as quickly drew back.

'I must not come too near you. Your grandfather sought so to comfort me. His touch broke the barrier. I could not release him. I did not know how. Never, then, could he return to his earth-wife and children.'

An enormous thought-question surfaced in Ia's mind: Su Su answered it.

'What happened to his earth-body? Why, just what had happened to mine. Bodies are made of millions and millions of atoms, are they not? It is as if ... what is that game you play with many pieces of stiff paper?'

'Playing-cards, you mean?' flashed Ia.

'Yes, those, as if the body atoms are shuffled in the same way into another combination, all the same atoms, yet different.'

'Sort of juggled around!' Ia felt severely shaken. Su Su's fan sent reviving air to her.

'Just so, tying us to these Gardens forever, thought-man and thought-woman. We wished so much to send comfort to his earth-wife, she you call Greengran. To do this, we united our thoughts, in an effort so powerful it broke the barriers between our worlds, but she did not understand the message; no one did. But that effort reduced the total of our atoms so that, never again can we repeat it.'

Ia looked wildly about her. *'That means he is still in here?'*

Su Su fanned her to calmness. 'Come, I will show him to you, although it will not be as clearly as you see me, for I do not have Chi Nu's strength to make him so.'

Ia crossed the tree-trunk bridge, behind Su Su, light-headed, then along the pathway leading to the banks of the tiny waterfall. There, Su Su halted beside one of the stone water god figures, raising her slanting black eyes to look into his — *Greengranpa's stone eyes.*

~

Cold water slashed Ia's face. Blinking it from her lashes, she saw water droplets drip from her grandfather's stone hands. Su Su held his elbow, pulled him back.

'Not too close, Thought-Husband, she must stay free.'

The grain of the stone widened, lost that dense solidity, became more shadowy, until Ia knew the little beard, peaked cap, jaunty stance and large dark eyes. A smile of relief lifted the corners of his lips. Ia felt her own lips curve in delight. The small, nervous-tick wriggle beneath her eye stopped.

'Thought-Husband feared for you.' Su Su looked closely at Ia. 'It is well with you now? We will talk. For we three, it is difficult: My thoughtwave is *yours*, Ia, and Thought-Husband's is *mine*, but his is not for you.' Ia's Granpa nodded, or shook his head, as Su Su explained, using such droll facial expressions that Ia's confusion dissolved into a laughing fit. 'So,' continued Su Su,' I will be for you both a — what is it? — to hold in one's hand and speak?'

'A telephone?' Ia could only suppose that was what Su Su meant.

The three-way conversation worked fluently and flexibly, their exchanging thoughts simply conveyed and understood, its main theme that they had patiently waited for her to visit Garriphouca ever since Su Su became aware that Ia shared her thoughtwave. That was the day she discovered Ia's hallway picture of Garriphouca to be another, weaker, communication tool. Since Ia's Garriphouca arrival, they had made urgent plans, keenly aware that no one but she could open the closed doors of her grandmother's mind, doors slammed shut the day her husband vanished.

'Yes,' transmitted Greengranpa through Su Su, 'that's what your grandmother thinks, not the amnesia-forgetting I'm supposed to have had, according to all her friends and neighbours. She will never know I never meant to leave her, unless you help us.'

Su Su interflashed him: 'From that day, Ia, she did not trust the love of men. Only if those doors of her mind open can that trust be found again. Only on that day will she step the pathway of peace and happiness once more.'

'Or us,' sighed Greengranpa, via Su Su. 'To do this we need your help.'

'But how? What can *I* do?'

Self-doubt swept over Ia like a deluge. Her knees weak, she sat on the grassy lawn beside the waterfall. Her granpa squatted on his hunkers before her, switching to a grin as he dived a hand into his jacket pocket, scurrying around in it until he found what it sought. Out it came. Slowly, his hand unfolded. On its palm lay a gold earring, a chubby Cupid figure, complete with bow and arrow. He placed it upside down on a nearby stone. Ia picked it up and read the tiny lettering on its reverse side: July 18th.

'This is one of the earrings she wore that day. Its hook worked loose so she took it off and put it in my pocket to keep it safe.'

'What's July the 18th?'

'The day of our marriage in your world.'

Ia's breath sucked in. 'Now I *am* sure.' Her thoughts

trickled: 'I love Greengran, you know that, and now, er, I love you and Su Su, and I do see how you got sort of *exiled* here to live together for always and always.' A thought niggled her. 'But you don't *look* old enough to be anyone's grandfather, and anyone would think Su Su was around seventeen.'

Sunshine fetched gleams from her grandfather's beard and sparkles from Su Su's jewelled hair sticks. Greengranpa rose to his feet, grabbed Su Su's pale hands in his big fist, exchanging quick, wry glances with her.

'It seems people stay whatever age they are when they enter our thought-world.' He gave Ia time to absorb this. 'And so,' he rolled his eyes teasingly, 'as I'm only twenty-five it feels peculiar to be a grandfather. Can't you call me something else?'

A friendly warmth swam in the air between them. Ia rolled her eyes, too, liking him enough to be cheeky.

'What, for instance?'

'I don't know.'

Su Su knew. 'Maybe, Pa-Pa-Twice?'

'Oh, brilliant, Su Su! How about that, er, Pa-Pa-Twice?'

'As you so rightly say, Ia, it's brilliant.' He swept off his cap and bowed to Su Su.

Ia made to replace the earring on the stone but Su Su shook her head. 'Keep it safely, it is important to our plan.'

Ia slipped it into her jeans pocket. 'What plan?'

She was shocked when they told her that she must coax her grandmother to come to the Japanese Gardens. That was all! Then, once she was inveigled inside, Su

Su, with Ia acting as a booster, would transmit the all-important message from Pa-Pa-Twice that he had not abandoned her: his earth-love for her had been true. Greengran, of course, would not be able to see either Su Su or Pa-Pa-Twice. Later on, too, she would come to understand the long-ago message they had transmitted. How Ia was to break the long silence about the Japanese Gardens was not explained to her.

'You will find a way,' thought-said Su Su. 'The boy who waits outside the Gate of Forgetfulness must help you with this.'

'You mean I can tell him? *Everything*?'

Su Su nodded: 'Go to him now, then return to us with the answer you find together. We will go to the Tea House to wait for this.'

~

Tully jumped violently at Ia's touch.

'Don't tell me you've come back! You've been hours. I thought you'd never come out, even Spud and Spalpeen were fidgeting. I've been worried sick, if you must know. I was going to see what you were up to, promise or no promise, as soon as the kiosk man came back — he's on his lunch break — and I've eaten nearly everything by the way — and then I sort of dropped off somehow.' Tully heaved a breath and stopped glaring. 'Aren't you hungry? You look very, er, well, bright. What happened? Anything? Nothing?'

'How can I get a word in with you going on like that?' Ia foraged in the lunch box. 'I'm starving.' She took a bit of cheese, then some apple, mixing their flavours with great satisfaction. 'What do you mean, I look bright? What way, bright?'

'Like you know something I don't. Do you?'

'Yes.' She poured milk into the flask cup and drained it. Then she dug the earring from her pocket and showed it to him.

'Where did you get that? It looks like something Greengran would wear.'

'I got it in there,' she said, 'near the little waterfall, and it *is* hers.'

'You found it, just like that? How could it be there after all these years? How do you know it's hers? Anyone could have lost it.'

'I *know* it's hers, Tully. I've been having a pretty peculiar time in there. You might have trouble believing it all, so we'd better go somewhere we won't be interrupted. Are the donkeys OK?' Ia clicked back the flask cup and snapped on the lid of the plastic lunch box.

'Huh.' Tully's eyes held hers a long moment. 'Well, there's the Garden of Eternity. I've been trying to guess what it's like, and we wanted to go there anyway. Come on, the donkeys are OK. I've found them another grazing spot up the lane. Here ... here, *you* take the earring. I'd hate to lose it, whoever it belongs to.'

'It *is* Greengran's,' she repeated, in the still air of the Garden of Eternity. They leaned on the rustic railing of a small viewing dais.

'It's a funny garden,' said Tully.

'Mm.'

'It's like Teresa's, really.'

'Mm.'

Just an area of untrodden gravel, raked and swirled

into intricate patterns, exactly as Teresa's was; odd, interestingly shaped rocks rested here and there, a tree, a shrub or two, stone seating overlooking it. Nothing much, and yet, and yet ...

'It's super quiet,' said Tully.

'Eternity might be quiet, I suppose,' said Ia.

'Is it a good place to tell me whatever it is?'

'Yes.'

'Well, tell me, then.'

'You're not going to believe it,' she began.

His playwriter's mind pounced upon the astonishing events as eagerly as a dog snaps up a bone: a real life play, the plot thickening, unravelling, thickening again, scene after scene, the last act put into his, er, their, hands to be worked at, worked out, and the climax, the end, would ... well, most of that would depend on Green-gran. His face lit up. 'I've had a brain wave ... we *can* make Greengran come. 'Suppose,' he said, spacing his words, 'suppose you hadn't come out just now, and that I'd gone in and couldn't find you, like, like ... then I'd have to run home and tell her, wouldn't I?'

'That would be *cruel*.'

'You've heard about being cruel to be kind, haven't you? Can you come up with a better idea?'

'Let me think.'

Long, long pause.

'Well?'

'Well, *maybe* ...'

'There isn't any other way. Come on. Let's work it out.'

The somewhat intricate plan finished itself as they walked the last few yards to the Gate of Forgetfulness.

But before anything else, they had to know if Su Su could organise it.

'You'd better run back in there and find out. Hurry, Ia, before the kiosk keeper comes back and gets suspicious, though I think he's half asleep most of the time, as a matter of fact.'

Ia rotated the fat Cupid between thumb and forefinger, her mind only half made up, time ticking the seconds.

'Here's the earring,' she said, all of a gasp. 'You won't lose it, will you? You'll take care of it?'

'Stop worrying. You know I won't lose it. Now, go inside. Check everything with your Su Su person and Granpa, Pa-Pa-Twice, I mean. I won't move until you get back.'

In a way, Tully had the toughest part. If the plan worked, Ia would have nothing much to do until later. Tully opened the Gate of Forgetfulness a few inches, pushed her through.

'Go on,' he whispered, squinnying through the narrow gap. That was Ia's territory.

She didn't need to go as far as the Tea House. They waited for her on the arching scarlet bridge. Su Su received Ia's thoughts yards away, her fan fluttering in agitation. Pa-Pa-Twice pursed and wriggled his lips.

Su Su's thoughts stilled: 'The boy's idea is good. It is the only way, yet taking you into our world is dangerous, even for so short a time.'

Ia sent a cautious, rechecking query: 'It will be all right, won't it, Su Su, as long as neither of you touches me?'

'Especially you and me, Ia.' Her granpa's eyes held

regret. 'I might find that a bit hard myself.'

'And I must not thought-call you here too strongly,' said Su Su, 'or Tully could not think you back again when he comes with Earth-Wife. Tell him Su Su agrees. First, he must look for you on the Island of Joy and Wonder. If he cannot see you then everything is well: you have crossed into our world. Next, he must hurry and we must wait.'

Well, that part is fixed all right, thought Ia, running to the Gate of Forgetfulness on shaking legs. Without telling a single lie, Tully can report that I went into the Japanese Gardens by myself, and did not come out, that I can't be found.

Tully poked his face around the Gate at the sound of her thudding feet. Until this second, everything had seemed airy-fairy, a plot for a play, but now, well, now...

'It's fixed,' she gasped. 'Bring Greengran to the water-fall, but remember *you're to call me back before anything else*. Promise?'

Tully's black eyes looked blacker because his cheeks had gone white. 'I promise.' His gasp was loud.

A sudden thought jerked at Ia's mind like a magnet. It was Su Su.

'Come!' it commanded.

Chapter 10

Ia ran towards Pa-Pa-Twice, her arms held out, eager to hug and hold this man, who looked more real now than her own father.

'No!' Su Su's sharp reminder stopped her dead. It would have been so *easy*.

'Coo-er, *my hands*.' Ia checked the rest of her body and teetered on the edge of panic. 'I'm *smoke*.'

'Steady now, don't do another faint.' Pa-Pa-Twice backed away, smiling. 'Su Su can't bring you too far in, that's all it is.'

'You're able to talk to me directly, without Su Su!'

'Yes, my dear, as long as you are in our world, I can, and there's plenty to talk about, all your life, mine, my children, Krik and Muna, so much, so much.'

They stood on the Island of Joy and Wonder. Su Su, smiling and happy, leaned against a pergola post looking more relaxed and natural than Ia had ever seen her.

'We might as well sit down,' said Ia's twenty-five-year-old grandfather. He sat on the stumpy end of the tree-trunk bridge, pointing her to a comfortable looking rock beside it. He jerked a thumb at the Hill of Ambition. 'Look, there's the boy,' he exclaimed. 'We will soon know if Su Su has thought you in far enough.'

'Tully!' shouted Ia, frightened.

Tully turned away, unseeing, unhearing. She heard his running feet grow fainter, fainter, and then the soft click of a gate closing. Her heartbeats heaved disconcerting thumps. Was she going crackers? Or would she wake up any minute and find everything just ordinary?

Click, click, click. Fast, sharp finger snapping penetrated the fuzz in Ia's head and checked her jitters. Pa-Pa-Twice massaged his fingers to ease them after so much action.

'I'm scared,' she said to him, gulping in air from Su Su's fan.

'Of course you are, my dear, and it's my fault. I should have remembered the terrible shock it was the first time someone didn't see me when I saw them.'

'Forgive us, Ia,' said Su Su. 'Do not be afraid. Soon Tully will come again for you.'

Their concern restored Ia. Her insides righted.

'You two talk now,' said Su Su, 'I go to prepare tea and rice cakes.'

She moved towards the Tea House, kimono and gown a kaleidoscope of colours. Pa-Pa-Twice read the niggle in Ia's mind. 'Thought-tea and thought-cakes taste as good here as the real thing outside,' he said. 'Now, tell me ...'

~

'Come *on*, Spalpeen!'

Fast movement was the only way Tully could keep the sinking void within him at bay as he replayed his inch-by-inch survey of the Island of Joy and Wonder. Had Ia been somewhere else all the time? She couldn't have been kidding him along, could she? No, she wasn't like that. But such things don't happen, not in this day and age, or do they? But the earring — she had found that earring and, and here it was in his pocket; he could feel it there. He took a long breath. Greengran's reactions will fix things, one way or the other.

'Come *on*, Spalpeen!'

Galvanised by Tully's urgent heels digging into his ribs, Spalpeen trotted on smoothly, tucking away the miles to Garriphouca. Teresa stopped dead halfway down the avenue, watching them coming, her chins wobbling from the jolt.

'Where's Ia, and that Spud?' said she.

'I, er ... where's Greengran?' Tully had no time for diversions.

'She's up in the house. I said, where's ...'

Tully urged Spalpeen forward: 'I have to tell her something,' he shouted.

Teresa whirled round, stared after him and broke into a puffing walk. What's he up to, that boy? she asked herself. Tell her — tell her what? 'Douglas!' she shouted to a bent figure in the potato field beyond the trees. 'Come down from there, Douglas, come down this minute.'

Douglas shuffled into what might have been a speedy run some years ago and caught her up outside the dining-room window. 'Bethehokey, Teresa,' he panted irritably, noticing Spalpeen, riderless, his rope reins hanging loose, nibbling at the lawn's grassy stubble.

'Sh!' She quelled him. 'Don't let the Mistress see ye.'

The 'Mistress' had pushed her farm accounts to one side and risen to her feet, facing Tully. She seemed to be suffering an attack of near-total deafness.

'*Whai* did you say?'

'I, er, said, there's a, em, er, a message waiting for you at the Japanese Gardens.' Having to repeat the sentence ruined Tully's calm act.

'Have you gone mad, Tully?' Her face had a grey look. One hand held her throat. Her voice sprayed him like ice-water.

'Please! Listen!' Tully felt aghast at what he had to do.

'I will not listen! No one here, *no one*, speaks of that dreadful place to me. You, you ...'

She stopped, still as stone, hypnotised by the earring in the palm of Tully's hand, the pupils of her eyes dilating into flat black discs. Her shaking fingers took the little figure from him. She swallowed, repeatedly.

'You have been in my room, Tully. How dare you!'

'No, no! I haven't been in your room.'

'Then you are a liar too, and we'll soon prove it.' Anger flared her cheeks. 'Go upstairs and get my mosaic box from the dressing table, now, this moment.'

'I'm not a liar, Greengran, you'll see. I'll get the box for you, I'll be back in two ticks.'

Douglas and Teresa looked at one another in high alarm. What now? What next? They watched Greengran pick the earring from her hand, set it down upon the rich gleam of the mahogany table, never removing her eyes from it until Tully burst back through the door, the jewellery box in his hand.

'There,' he said, tensely.

She lifted the lid and tipped the earrings into a glittering heap several inches away from that single gold one. Greengran's intake of breath hissed. Tully poked a hesitant forefinger into the tiny heap. He extricated a second fat Cupid and pushed it along the table to join its twin. *One pair*. He felt distinctly odd. Every doubt he had fled.

'I ... don't ... understand.' Greengran swayed.

Jumping towards her, Tully caught sight of the two faces shadowing the window pane. 'Help, help!' he yelled. By the time Teresa and Douglas cannoned into the dining room, Greengran sat erect, having ordered herself to do so by dint of will. Her face was colourless.

'Look, Teresa,' she said, and pointed to the two Cupids. She made no explanation or comment.

'We saw through the window,' Teresa admitted. 'I've been telling Douglas they're the very same earrings ye had on the day ...' Her eyes were round, foreboding, her breathing heavy.

'The day my husband abandoned me.' Greengran completed the sentence, using a flat, cold, positive voice.

'Bethehokey, ma'am, bethehokey, now, well, bethehokey ...'

'Don't be saying that, ma'am. We won't be talking about that time at all, at all.' Teresa glared at Tully. 'If that boy has upset ye, I'll give him a good smacking, big and all as he is. We shouldn't have told them, I shouldn't have let them see, but they *promised* — it's all my fault.' Savagely, she switched again to Tully. 'And that Ia, where *is* she? Wait until I see that one, I'll ...'

'Do stop, Teresa. What are you saying? I'm utterly confused. Where is Ia, Tully? And where did you find *this*? Tell me again what you said just now, about the Japanese Gardens, I mean? And what is all your fault, Teresa? What have you done?'

'Bethehokey, yiz are all in a terrible tiz. Sit down, will yiz, sit down this minute,' said Douglas. Each obeyed Douglas instantly, half-expecting one of his swearing attacks, hoping to avert it. 'Now, ma'am,' he continued, 'I'm afraid Teresa and myself might have told the children too much yisterday but, sure, didn't their own parents take it into their heads to tell them a good lot, a few days since, and weren't they mad to know the rest. It seemed better to keep them on the right track, so ...' He brought Greengran as far as the children's planned second visit to the Japanese Gardens.

'I accept your explanation, Douglas,' said Greengran, 'and thank you, thank you both. Knowing as much as that, it is only natural they should be curious, of course, but this, this ...'

'That little gold fella,' Teresa whispered.

'Now, then, boyo,' Douglas scowled at Tully, 'it's your turn for explaining. There ye are dancing about as if ye'd ants in your pants.'

'She sort of found it, Ia, I mean, er, beside the little waterfall in the Japanese Gardens, she said. She ran out with it in her hand and told me to show it to Greengran and make her come. Then she went back inside, and ...' Tully spoke in spurts.

'You mean you've let her go back in there *alone*?' Greengran's voice grated.

'Well, yes, because she said she had to, and, and ...'

Silence filled every corner of the room like transparent cement.

'And what?'

'... and she is still in there, Greengran. When she didn't come back I went inside and looked and looked and looked. I couldn't find her.' Tully's breath jerked. There, not one lie told.

'No! Oh, no, no, no, *no*.'

Greengran's cry sliced him like a razor. Ia was right to call his so-called clever idea out-and-out cruel, but it was too late to change anything. He forced himself on: 'You see, Ia had discovered something. The earring is supposed to tell you that. She says you have to come back with me to find out what it is. I didn't tell anyone about her not coming out because I know she is in there; she *has* to be.'

Douglas looked as pole-axed as the others but he carried on as decisively as before.

'We'll all go, ma'am,' he said, 'Mr Krik, and us, and Micky and Ferna O'Mara had better come. They might be a help or they might be a hindrance, ye niver can tell with them two. I'll be off now to fetch Mr Krik. Tully, run to the O'Maras, no, you'd better telephone. Say to meet us at their gate on the ponies: they'd be handy for looking where the van can't be driving. And take Spalpeen's bridle off and put him into the field while ye are waiting for meself and your uncle. We'll be back in no time, Mrs Fairley, ma'am.'

'You are quite right, Douglas, you are always at your best in emergencies, we both are. Get hold of Krik, say we need his van-jeep thing, my Mini is too small for all of us, but try and get him over the shock first. We don't want him driving us into a ditch on the way. Hurry.' She turned to Teresa. 'Help me to change my earrings,' she said, 'I shall wear these.'

'Ia said the fastening isn't safe,' said Tully.

Greengran examined it: 'I remember now,' she said, softly, 'but wear them I must.' Her stiff lips tried to smile. 'I'm sorry I was angry with you, Tully, and I'm glad you didn't tell anyone else about Ia disappearing, er, I mean still being in that, that dreadful place. Time enough if, if ...'

Tully ran to telephone the O'Maras.

~

A gong sounded from the Tea House: Su Su's interflash overrode Ia's fluent transmission of family tidings to Pa-Pa-Twice.

'Come to tea. There is good news. Hurry.'

They jumped up, reaching out affectionate hands, one to the other, until, at the last split second, Pa-Pa-Twice remembered and jerked his swiftly back as if stung.

'That was a near miss, Pa-Pa-Twice!'

He nodded wryly, wrenching his smile into action. 'Race you to the Tea House,' he challenged. Ia ran at top speed and was considerably astounded to arrive at the Tea House unpuffed. Pa-Pa-Twice chuckled, reading her mind.

'Thought-running doesn't puff,' he said.

'Small-Boy Thought-Husband likes playing tricks,' remarked Su Su to Ia, a smile twitching her butterfly-shaped lips.

Ia checked her run across the veranda when she saw Pa-Pa-Twice take off his shoes, placing them alongside Su Su's wooden sandals by the open door. She slipped off her own sandals, adding them to the line. The act gave her immense satisfaction, heightened when Su Su's lacquer-black head bowed in approval.

'What good news, Su Su?' asked Ia.

'Thought-Husband's Earth-Wife will come,' replied Su Su. 'It was difficult for me to understand at first — I could see these people, not read their thoughts, but I think Tully's plan works well.'

'You have been Ghost-Ladying at Garriphouca,' gasped Ia. 'I wish I could do that. When is she coming?'

'Soon. Everyone runs about: Douglas, Teresa, even your uncle — he does not often hurry without his wheels, does he? — and Tully seeks two children to ride ponies.'

'The O'Maras. Gosh,' said Ia, 'they're not all coming, are they? You wanted Greengran to come alone, didn't you?'

'Tully helps your grandmother to understand this but the other people wish to care for her. But they will obey her, do not worry.'

Su Su sank to her knees, sitting back on her heels on one of three flat and gleaming cushions scattered on the floor near a low, low table, her kimono arranged her in shining folds. 'Let us celebrate the Tea Ceremony together,' she said, and gestured Pa-Pa-Twice and Ia to join her.

Pa-Pa-Twice's ordinary clothing did not allow him Su Su's grace but his flexing knees showed long practice as he criss-crossed them, buddha fashion. Ia folded her legs on the third cushion, her mind washed free of past and future events, as Su Su intended.

Su Su lifted a bamboo tea scoop and its container, a small ceramic bowl, and put two and a half scoopfuls of tea for each of them into the bowl, then took a ladleful of hot water from a pretty kettle sitting on top of a small metal brazier, poured one third of it into the bowl and returned the remainder to the kettle. Then, she used a stubby bamboo whisk to whip it into a foamy green mixture, which took some time, and she concocted each little bowlful of tea individually. The whole thing enthralled Ia, even though she was not as fascinated by the tea's taste. The tiny rice cakes resting on a paper napkin in front of her cushion were delectable. She wished she could have more, that she did not need to be so Japanese-polite. Su Su turned her head suddenly, rose to her feet. Powerful and confusing thoughtwaves approached.

'Your world's time runs alongside us now, Ia,' she said. 'Go with Thought-Husband to the waterfall where our message is prepared. Listen well to his instructions. When Tully calls you away from us, it is you two who must lead Earth-Wife to understanding.'

Pa-Pa-Twice stared at Su Su: 'I feel nervous suddenly, Thought-Wife. What if ...? I mean, it's been so long. I ...'

'Earth-Wife will discover our gift. It is more golden than the god-of-love earrings,' she said.

They looked deeply into one another, forgetting that Ia shared in their mingling thoughts. The pure white flash of thought-love between them made an inward mark upon her which time would never erase.

Pa-Pa-Twice braced his body: 'Come to the waterfall, Ia,' he said. 'I'll show you what's what.'

'Are you not coming, Su Su?'

'Soon, but first I will be Ghost Lady and watch for Earth-Wife and Tully. Perhaps Tully needs my help. If it is possible, I shall try to give him this.'

~

Tully's only needs, however, appeared to be prayer offerings for his safety or, maybe, a pill for travel sickness; Uncle Krik had left the Rathcur grasslands roadway in favour of direct, cross-country driving, aiming the half-van-half-jeep like an arrow to the Japanese Gardens. His mother had said 'Hurry!' hadn't she? Krik's van-jeep threatened to break apart as he hurled it over ruts, rabbit holes and hard, grass-hidden humps. His passengers clutched window handles, seat backs, cushions, anything, for anchorage. Tully felt his bones crackle and crunch but being wedged between Greengran and Teresa kept him seated. The bumps and bounces jounced all protesting cries into unintelligible grunts. Krik closed his ears to one and all. He could not abide back-seat drivers. Occasionally, through the leaping wing mirror, Tully glimpsed the O'Maras in the distance, ponies at full gallop. The interior driving mirror featured Greengran's earring Cupids frantically disco-dancing.

I wish I could stop my teeth from gritting together, Tully thought, but if they were not gritting, I suppose they would be rattling. He felt his sense of humour making a faint comeback; Teresa gave an electrifying shriek as Krik drove straight for grass bank looming ahead like a giant horse-show ditch.

'Bethehokey!' roared Douglas.

Everyone plunged their heads into their hands, including Uncle Krik. The van-jeep's whirling wheels cleared the last blades of grass and touched down in several thumps. Krik instinctively wrenched at the steering wheel, braking violently.

'You can sit up now,' he shouted, 'I've hit the road just right. We're nearly there.'

'Bethehokey,' Douglas unwound himself from his crouch in the front passenger seat, 'I thought we were gone entirely.'

'That Krik, ma'am,' Teresa gasped, a speck of colour diluting her milk-white face, 'he is the worst driver in the whole world.' Her plump hands grasped Douglas's horny ones.

'Maybe he is the best, in a strange sort of way.' Greengran gazed downhill to the tall, pale wood palisade encircling the Japanese Gardens. Uncle Krik aimed the van-jeep into the Garden's car park, jerking it to a halt two inches short of a hefty tree trunk.

'Everyone out,' he said, not moving. *'You're* supposed to be in charge from here on, Tully. I'll stay at the wheel, ready to chase around if need be. The O'Maras can wait with me here when they arrive. They can cover the rough ground by pony better than I can.'

'No one is to make a fuss,' said Tully. The authority in his voice surprised himself. Tremors shivered through Greengran's body, freeing his own fears. 'We have to act ordinary, you see,' he said to Douglas. 'The kiosk man is not to know there is anything odd going on. He'll be there by now, I should think.'

'Yiz are not going in there by yourselves,' butted in Teresa.

'Only Greengran and me go inside,' repeated Tully.

'Well!' said Teresa.

'Just buy our tickets at the kiosk, Greengran,' said Tully, 'and I'll make some joke about coaxing my Granny to come.'

'Tully is so sure about, about, about ... well, it must be all right.' Greengran stood stiffly. 'Wait nearby, all of you. We'll find Ia, don't you worry, and she will, she will ...'

'She'll show you what she's found inside the Gardens!' said Tully.

Chapter 11

'It's a different kiosk man,' Tully gasped his relief.

'Thank Heaven for that,' Greengran said. 'Let's be quick in case the other one comes back.'

Both had steadied, now that action had begun. They saw it in each other, put more trust in the other. Greengran bought entry tickets, making casual remarks as to the state of the weather.

'It's been a grand day,' agreed the man, 'but you've missed the best of it for the Gardens. You've only the half hour left, but you'll have it to yourselves anyway.'

'Oh, I'm sure that will be long enough for us.' Greengran flashed her charming smile, the one like a lighthouse beam.

Oh, boy, can she put on an act! Tully nearly applauded the show of airy nonchalance. But Greengran dropped her role the moment the Gate of Forgetfulness closed behind them. She stood rock-still, as Ia had done, but with an air of purpose, as if fitting on and adjusting a mental crash helmet against possible head wounds. Her eyes closed. She drew deep, deep breaths. Tully adjusted his own fast breathing. It helped.

'Did you say the waterfall?' she asked then, eyes fully open, reflecting dark-green shadows cast by curiously-shaped conifer trees.

He nodded.

'I remember the way,' she said.

Tully trailed her methodical steps, stopping, restarting, in a meditation so profound he was afraid to break into it, yet a-dance in nervous trepidation. At this rate, they would never get there. Hurry, hurry, hurry! At last, the Marriage Bridge. Go on, go on, he inwardly urged her, again and again. *Go on.*

'Why did I stay away so long?'

Tully only heard her whisper because of the all-embracing quietude; even the stream rippled soundlessly over the coins on its gravelled bottom. His impatience ebbed. The knot in his stomach unwound a little when he saw the five penny piece Ia had dropped in.

'Did *you* drop in a coin, you and ...?'

Greengran fingered aside a tear so fast he thought he imagined it. She gave a small nod, a half smile, blinked twice. 'Yes, yes, we did. That one there, the gold one.'

'We were wondering about that gold one, me and Ia. Would you like to have it back? I could easily get it.'

'No. Leave it there. That is not the discovery, is it? Or this?' She touched a Cupid earring.

'No, the discovery is sort of out-of-this-world, as a matter of fact, and, well ... come on. Hurry.'

Foreboding seized Tully again. His hands went cold

and sweaty. They felt slippery holding the rail of the
little bridge. His stress infected Greengran.

'Are you sure Ia will come? Quite sure?'

How could he answer that, he thought. 'Come
quickly,' he said instead.

Suspense dogged them along the Hill of Ambition's
pathways and jagged steep steps. They reached the
stone seat overlooking the Island of Joy and Wonder.
Greengran sat on it, panting.

'Phew, I'm getting too ancient for this, Tully.'

'You're not ancient,' he said, 'but stay there just the
same, I'll be back in a couple of minutes, er, *we'll* be
back.'

She gave Tully a penetrating stare but said nothing.
He tore on towards the waterfall, his mind beating out
Ia's name to the thuds of his feet — Ia, Ia, Ia. But only
the stone gods peopled the bare spaces by the waterfall.
His inner cry wailed like a siren. 'Ia, come back. Come
back. You've got to come back!' The bones of his legs
threatened to dissolve.

~

A thump between his shoulder blades swung Tully
about.

'Ia! Divil mend you, where have you *been*?'

'I've been walking around you in circles, haven't I?
Why did you take no notice of me yelling at you just
now?' Ia's irritability betrayed her strain.

'I never saw you, and I didn't hear you either, I
thought you'd never come. You had me in a terrible
sweat.' His sentences jerked out in spasms. 'Hey, you're

kind of vague-looking, er, I mean, not properly *solid*.'

'Oh, am I? I forgot to check that. You should have seen me a while back. Oh, no, you couldn't, could you, I was all smoke really.'

'*Smoke*?' Tully was aghast.

'Well, sort of. I'll explain later.' She examined her body. 'I think it must take a couple of minutes to get completely normal. See? I'm pretty OK now, aren't I? And no wonder you didn't hear me, I was only thinking, not talking.'

'What are you talking about?'

'In there is not like out here, Tully,' she said.

'But it *is* the same place, isn't it?'

'It is and it isn't,' she said.

'Huh,' he said, nonplussed. 'Was it awful, or what?'

'No, it wasn't awful.'

Tully surveyed her minutely — did she sound sorry to be back? Ia gave him one quick glance, then re-met his eyes with a startled, doubletake intensity. Don't be silly, she told herself.

'What about Greengran?' she asked. 'Is she all right? She hasn't gone funny or anything, has she?' She was relieved when Tully shook his head. 'That's something, but what is the idea of all the others coming? Uncle Krik to drive is OK but Teresa *and* Douglas *and* the O'Maras as well, why?'

'How do you know they're here?'

'I know,' she said.

'They won't make any fuss, they've promised, and nobody else knows. They just came in case ... well, in case.'

A pause.

'Are you sure Greengran's all right? Where is she? I missed out on that by doing my change-back.'

'Apart from being a bit puffed she's fine. She's getting her wind back on that seat near the Island of Joy and Wonder.'

Ia guessed Su Su would keep an eye on her grandmother there. 'Listen, Tully,' she said, 'I'll tell you as fast as I can what we are to do, and then we'll go and fetch her.'

Without Su Su and Pa-Pa-Twice to support her, Ia's confidence evaporated even as she told him: what if the repercussions of their act should unhinge Greengran and not open her mind to happiness after all? Tully watched her lips tremble.

'I hope it is going to work, Tully.'

'Well, tell me whatever it is. Get it over.' He fidgeted.

'I suppose you have your notebook and pencil?'

'Of course, I have, but why? What is that to do with anything?'

'You might need the notebook to practise in, that's why.

'What do you mean, practise? Practise what?'

'Come over here a minute, I'll show you,' she said, and moved over to the stone water-god, where the stepping stones began, touching its stone hand with hers.

It took Tully longer than a minute to get the hang of it. Everything felt like being in some sort of play, half written by himself in a confusing way, except it wasn't.

'Come on,' Ia said, 'let's get it over. Let's fetch Greengran.'

~

'Oh, so there you are, Ia,' Greengran said, coolly, ignoring the oddity of everything. 'You have a good deal of explaining to do, you know. To put it mildly, you have caused a lot of trouble and inconvenience ...'

'You're wearing both earrings! He'll be so pleased.' Ia leaned over the stone bench, curling her arms around her grandmother's shoulders.

'He? Who?' Greengran grasped at control, paling. 'Now, Ia, let's be sensible, shall we? I don't really know what has got into you. It's not at all like you to behave as you're doing, worrying me into a fit because I thought you would, well, perhaps not *be* here when I came, and here you are all the time and playing rather a cruel trick. Tully told me you found this earring (her fingers flew to check it) and somehow guessed it might be mine, even after all these years ...'

'I didn't guess, Greengran, and I didn't find it. He gave it to me.'

'Who is this *he*? One of the gardeners, perhaps? And what is all this about something you are supposed to have discovered, the reason for my coming here, in fact? It had better be good, Ia.'

The sharp asperity of her grandmother's voice and her bread-white face made Ia ache. 'Sit down again, Greengran, I'll tell you everything, if you promise to listen. I'm not being cruel, honestly, it's because I love you, all of us do. What I have to tell you *is* very peculiar, but it will soon be over and then you'll be glad. Now, will you listen?'

'I suppose, as I have come this far, I'll have to,' said

Greengran, feeling Ia's kind hands.

'Er, you remember,' began Ia, well aware of the dangerous ground she was about to tread, 'you remember about Greengranpa's Ghost Lady, don't you? Well ...' She spoke for several minutes.

Then.

'Thoughtwaves, Chi Nu, Su Su, Thought-Husband, Earth-Wife! Your imagination has run riot. Garriphouca and this, er, *place*, must have gone to your head.' Greengran was not pale now. She was crimson. 'Your parents should have known better than to rake up the past to you like that.'

'But what about that earring?' Tully broke in, determined to keep to what he saw as the point.

'Coincidence, nothing else, you'd better put it in one of your plays.' Greengran's voice was tart.

'It's a pity about the rest of the message,' Tully murmured.

'The rest of what message?'

'The earring is only half the message, I *told* you,' said Ia, 'Tully is going to help you with the other half, er, over at the waterfall.'

'The next bit of trickery, no doubt. I'm really worried by the fantasy world you two have built up between you; if I wasn't so worried, I would be extremely angry. Now, for goodness sake, let's get it over with, then we can go home.' Greengran leapt to her feet, striding off.

Ia ran after her, saying nothing, doubtful suddenly of everything she had seen and done today. *Had* her imagination got the better of her at last like Miss Porrage said it would? Well, she would know soon enough.

They stepped on to the grassy approach to the waterfall, saw a stone figure sitting on either side. Su Su stepped out of the figure on the far bank, radiantly colourful, smiling encouragingly, her fan poised. Exquisite relief flooded Ia's every pore. She had forgotten that Su Su used the water-goddess to rest in; it even looked faintly like her, the same way the water god beside her bore a shadow-likeness to Pa-Pa-Twice.

Tully nipped her elbow: 'Look at Greengran!' he hissed.

She seemed entranced by the blossoming trees' reflections shining in the dark water, the small foaming waterfall, the pathway to the Tea House, the water-gods — 'I don't remember ... these were not ... this statue wasn't ... I ....' — Greengran chewed at her bottom lip, rather as Ia sometimes did, shook her head, narrowed her eyes to look at the nearest water-god piercingly, giving a short metallic laugh. 'Oh, no, it's not possible. Now *I* am imagining things. Why, I can hardly remember *how* he looked, and yet ... oh, it's all so long ago.' Conflicting emotions criss-crossed her face — disbelief, bewilderment and confusion, doubt, wonder, wistful longing.

Ia caught Tully's eye, she nodded. It was time. Between them, they drew Greengran closer to the nearby stone figure.

'The message is on that,' said Ia. She pointed to a writing slate held by the carved stone hands. Vertical lines of unintelligible squiggles crowded the slate's surface.

'It's sort of the same as *my* made-up language.' Tully's voice oozed satisfaction. Greengran stared at him. 'How can that be?' she asked.

'I don't know how it can be,' he admitted, 'but it is.'

'It looks more like Japa ...' Again Greengran stopped short. She switched her stare to Ia for a long moment. 'Your thought-world is nonsense,' she said, her voice all of a quiver. 'Isn't it?'

'That writing is the other half of your message.' Ia leaned against her grandmother, lending strength. 'Let's sit on the grass, Greengran. Tully is going to translate it for you. He's been practising on the beginning part of it, then, if you want to, he will write an answer from you.'

'Now? Shall I read it now?' asked Tully.

'Very well.' Greengran's body stiffened. 'If you must.'

' "To my Earth-Wife, Sophia",' that is how it begins,' said Tully.

Believe Ia when she explains my new world to you,
Why I am here, why only she could visit me and Su Su.
Believe, too, that my earth-love for you did not fail.
My exile here, and our parting, was accidental.
Time does not exist in this thought-world, as in yours.
For all the earth years that have passed with you,
Your earring has remained in my pocket, where you
placed it.
That is the first proof I sent to you.
The second is lettered round the brim of the head band
worn by this statue.
Only you will understand it.

Tully's eyes, and Ia's too, flicked towards the lettering and away again, even Tully, this time, mystified by it. Not so Greengran. Her emerald-green eyes shone as brightly as the springing grass they sat on, and a new flush of blood vivified the pearly quality of her skin. Ia felt awed.

'She is beautiful,' she whispered.

'What does it say?' Tully wanted to know.

'It says Mizpah,' Greengran said. 'Finish reading the slate message, Tully.' Slow and gentle tears wet her cheeks. If the word had meaning, it seemed hers alone. Tully tucked it into the back of his mind for future reference, just the same. It was working, that was the main thing.

'There's not much left,' he said, turning back to his decoding:

> We must wish each other a different happiness, Sophia.
> Su Su gives this to me, and I to her.
> Your true happiness is not far from Garriphouca.
> Trust in it. Take it, gladly.
> When you have done so, come again to these Gardens and drop a new coin into the water.
> We shall know this and you will feel our presence.
> Give the Cupid earrings to Ia on her wedding day.

'Coo-er!' said Ia.

'Good idea.' Tully's smile flashed.

Gaiety cloaked Greengran from head to toe. 'I do want you to write my answer, Tully,' she said. 'Write this down.'

> My dear, (dictated Greengran). You have given me back myself. I am not able to experience your new world but I do believe all that Ia has told me of it. My blessing to you and Su Su. I know that I should also love her. I shall not refuse that other happiness. We will visit here many times

so that you both may see it.
Mizpah.
P.S. The earrings shall be Ia's when that day comes.

Tully finished writing, tore the page from his notebook and began inserting it into the hairline crack between the stone fingers and the writing slate. Suddenly, Greengran took the page from him.

'No,' she said, 'let me do that. I need to be alone here for a minute or two. You understand, don't you?'

'*I* do,' said Tully.

'Go outside and tell the others I won't be too long.'

'But ...' began Ia.

As they turned away, they glimpsed Greengran's hand stretch out to the stony one.

'*You* go on, Tully,' said Ia. 'Do what she said. I have to be by myself, too, just for a little while. (She was watching Su Su near the Tea House, heard her calling.) I have to say goodbye.'

Ia's bereft expression disturbed Tully but he nodded, aware of her need. 'Don't be long,' he said, and walked swiftly away.

Su Su's dark almond eyes followed Tully's every step until he had crossed the scarlet bridge, was out of their sight. She looked wistful. 'If I could be a grandmother, Ia, I think I would wish Tully for a grandson.'

'I could never imagine *you* a grandmother!' Ia saw Su Su sigh.

'So now you think a small goodbye, Ia?'

'You mean it needn't be for always?'

'Our thoughtwaves stay the same, do they not?'

'Yes ... but ...'

'You will return to Garriphouca, will you not?'

'Yes, whenever I can, but ...'

'It may be quite soon perhaps, maybe often.'

'Oh, I hope so, Su Su, but will you be there? And will you Ghost-Lady Garriphouca avenue to see *me*? What about Pa-Pa-Twice? What about *him*? You can't think me back into your thought-world ever again, I know that, but I could always come here to *see* you both, couldn't I?'

'Do this when important happenings enter your life, that will be the best way, just as your grandmother promises to show us her new happiness. Sometimes, too' — the thought-sound of Su Su's laugh was soft — 'I shall Ghost Lady the avenue when you are at Garriphouca, sometimes, too, the picture in your hallway at home. We wish a share in the earth lives of those we love, Thought-Husband and me.'

'I wish we could *all* be together, Su Su.'

'But it is not possible. Be happy, Ia, as we shall be.' Su Su half turned to greet Pa-Pa-Twice, suddenly beside her. 'Remember, we three were together once to make our gift of freedom and happiness to Earth-Wife.'

Pa-Pa-Twice nodded, his eyes delving into Ia's: 'Go now, Ia,' he said, transmitting through Su Su once more, 'go to your grandmother. All is well with her. We have you to thank for that, and Tully too.'

A query still squirmed about inside Ia. Su Su caught it.

'You do not yet understand why we used Tully's language to write our message? The answer will fall into your mind when you do not expect, exactly as our other, so-long-ago message to your world will one day come.

No one understood it then. No one else knew it. It is better this should be so.'

Pa-Pa-Twice held Su Su's pale hands in one of his, pressed the fingertips of the other to his lips and from them, very slowly, blew Ia a most tender kiss. Slower even than he, Ia repeated the mime, once to him, once to Su Su. She felt rent in two.

~

Warm hands held her: 'It's time to go, Ia,' Greengran murmured. 'They must be tired of waiting for us outside.'

Which, of course, they were, even Mr Clintlock, although he could not be said to be waiting exactly. Having barely dislodged himself from behind the steering wheel of a veteran Rolls Royce, he was rampaging towards the pale wood palisade, his bullet-shaped head lowered as if to butt down the fencing. Krik, Douglas, Teresa, Ferna and Micky, Mr and Mrs O'Mara, and Johnjoe scattered before him, all of them there because of Micky's mixed-up telling of Tully's phone call. Each one had sped off to look for Ia, dropping tasks in hand like stones. Mr Clintlock pranced across the final few feet just as Greengran slipped through the Gate of Forgetfulness.

'Sophia!' Mr Clintlock roared, his flailing arms swinging out, making her a stopping buffer. 'Sophia,' he said a second time, very quietly. His arms stayed around her.

Ia stood halfway in, halfway out, of the Gateway, halfway between its past and future threshold. Tully jerked her across it, into the present.

'Look,' he hissed, 'it's all working according to plan. What an end for a play!'

'Except it isn't a play, is it?' said Ia.

Chapter 12

Those who had waited outside did ask awkward questions but Greengran so beguiled them with white lies (she leaned heavily on the children's TV play plotting and playing) that they forgot to be critical.

'I was quite carried away by the whole thing,' she ended. 'Just wait until you see it yourselves on TV ... Tully and Ia are entering it for that young playwriters' competition, you know. It's bound to win.' Greengran remained encased within Mr Clintlock's grip. 'I am sorry you have been so worried. I was myself at first, but now,' triumph rang in her voice, 'well, now, your hush-hush days are over where I'm concerned. *I'm cured.* What is past is past, and that is that.' She smiled nonchalantly over Mr Clintlock's shoulder. 'The future is what is important.'

Ia's smile widened and deepened: that is *it*, or *going* to be it, Greengran's happiness, that is.

In silent accord, the rest of the group splintered,

wearing glowing expressions of relief and rejoicing. Mr Clintlock settled Greengran beside him on the blue leather seat before gliding away in his purring Rolls Royce. Mr and Mrs O'Mara sprang off at a gallop on their mane-flowing Arab stallions, hers snow white, his jet black. Uncle Krik and Johnjoe rattled back the way they came. Teresa and Douglas walked sturdily towards the Rathcur grasslands, undeterred by Teresa's wobbling hips and bosom. Fatigue swamped Ia. She found it hard to stir. Tully sensed her need.

'Come on,' he said, 'it's over, you know. Let's go home.'

'You two have a right nerve,' said Micky, scowling at them from Pooka's back, 'getting everyone here on false pretences. I thought we'd have to hunt all over the place for Ia or she would disappear for ever and ever, like that Mr Fairley.'

'Thanks,' said Ia.

'Oh, shut up, Micky, leave it alone, can't you, they both look whacked.' Ferna turned to Ia. 'Ia, you get on Shee and I'll have Spud again, then we can get going. You look after Tully, Micky.'

'It had better be good, that's all I can say,' muttered Micky.

'What had?' asked Tully.

'That so-called play of yours, if it ever does get on TV that is.'

'It will.' Ia sat slumped in Shee's saddle.

'Is it finished, Tully?' Ferna asked, 'I mean, all written down and everything?'

'The writing bit comes next,' admitted Tully, 'but it shouldn't take too long with Ia helping, then, if there is time before she has to go back to England, maybe the four of us could act it out and see how it sounds.'

Transferring the play from heads to paper proved distinctly laborious, a lot having to be omitted, some invented. Interruptions interfered with the work too, like Greengran and Mr Clintlock deciding to become engaged the day everyone went to Poolgorum, Mr Clintlock driving Jenny, the gennet, harnessed to the pony trap, instead of his Rolls Royce, and Krik staying home to oil and grease it for him as a kindness. Unfortunately, he misplaced the famous Rolls Royce purr when he had finished poking about in its internal combustion innards, which was embarrassing. He admitted later that only Rolls Royce people should really do anything to a Rolls Royce.

Mr Clintlock's engagement gift to Greengran astonished one and all — an electric generator for Garriphouca House. The struggle for stream power was over. Greengran even consented to visit the mill's water-wheel, fell under its spell, and forever afterwards wore Mr Clintlock's second gift, tiny water-wheel earrings.

Teresa retrieved (from some dark corner of a drawer) the 'bit of paper' certifying that she and Douglas had once been legally married. It was high time to finish the thing off properly, she said, and Douglas could buy her a wedding ring the very next day he was in the city, if he liked, and, bethehokey, he did.

Ferna and Micky came to Garriphouca House every day to check out the play's progress. Then, of course, Ia and Tully would need to rest for a while or visit Mrs Goodey, or go rafting on the pond, things like that ... anyway, it was hard work right up to the evening of the day before Ia had to go home. In the short space of time after breakfast, on that last morning the four of them gave the play a trial run through, in the hayloft. The result showed a need for alteration here and there to make it ring more truly, to scintillate as brightly as they knew it could. But how to do it? By letter? Hardly, the entry date of the competition was barely two weeks off. Greengran was consulted.

Her organisational ability flew into action, her scheme reaching finalisation fifty yards from Dublin Airport. By sheer luck, coincidence, call it what you will, Tully's parents were scheduled to touch down from the United States a bare half hour before Ia's departure time. If Greengran's plan worked, that Manchester flight would also be Tully's. As the New York plane landed a fraction behind time communication speed was of the essence, like greetings, explanations and why Tully should fly away with Ia instead of returning home with his parents. As Greengran gesticulated throughout all this with the air ticket she had already bought for their son, they had little choice. The fast reunion-farewell, parent-son-gabble-gabble turned into rush-rush to the Manchester departure gate.

During all this kerfuffle Ia stood transfixed, dumb-founded, her widened eyes hypnotised by Tully's mother, Cliona Carrigaline. She felt the floor's support weaken, become insubstantial, like a summer cloud. The puzzling clues, hints and pointers seen, heard and experienced during the last two weeks clanged into place like a line of lemons on a fun-fair fruit machine. *Cliona Carrigaline. She* was the long-ago message, the mysterious baby Teresa had reared, who married —

Tully's father! Blur. Blur.

'Come on. Stop hanging about.' Tully's voice.

'Goodbye, darling Ia.' Greengran's voice.

Tully gripping her elbow, pushing, pulling.

Tully shouting: '*Mizpah*, Greengran! I know what it means.'

Greengran blushing.

Hands waving.

Boarding the plane.

Taking off.

Ia's shocked state slid away as smoothly as the ground beneath the plane. She felt clean and new, like the gold and blue world outside the aircraft window.

'It says to unfasten your seat belt,' said Tully. 'We're on our way, sort-of-cousin.'

'Cousins-more-or-less, you mean.' Ia closed her eyes, smiling, her mind echoing Su Su's last words: 'No one understood it then. Tell no one now. It is better this should be so.' Ia flashed intensive thoughtwaves through the high thin air. Now *they* would know she knew! She opened her eyes. There was still one thing she did not know.

'Tully. What was that other thing you said? About *Mizpah*, I mean?'

'Oh, I didn't get a chance to tell you, did I? I remembered to look it up last night.'

'But what *does* it mean?'

'The Lord watch between me and thee when we are absent from each other. That's what it means,' said Tully. A satisfied expression showed in his Su Su-like, sloe-black eyes.

'Oh.' Ia's breath swooshed out. 'Brilliant!' she said.